BOOK 2
OF THE
NYMPH
SERIES

Montana
Mustangs

DANICA WINTERS
author of *The Nymph's Labyrinth*

Crimson Romance
New York London Toronto Sydney New Delhi

CRIMSON
ROMANCE

Crimson Romance
An Imprint of Simon & Schuster, Inc.
1230 Avenue of the Americas
New York, NY 10020

For information about special discounts for bulk purchases, please contact Simon & Schuster Special Sales at 1-866-506-1949 or business@simonandschuster.com.

The Simon & Schuster Speakers Bureau can bring authors to your live event. For more information or to book an event contact the Simon & Schuster Speakers Bureau at 1-866-248-3049 or visit our website at www.simonspeakers.com.

ISBN: 978-1-4405-6545-8
ISBN: 978-1-4405-6546-5 (ebook)

To Herb and Judy—

Thank you for your constant love and support.
You are such incredible people.
I'm honored to be considered one of your wonderful daughters.

Acknowledgments

To all men and women who work to protect our country, I want to thank you. Your hard work and sacrifices do not go unnoticed.

I must extend my sincerest thanks to the Missoula City Police Department for allowing me the honor of spending time with their officers. Your officer's professionalism, sincerity, kindness, and compassion are what make your department truly commendable.

A special thanks to Officer Mattix who took me on an educational and fun ride-along. That is one experience I will not soon forget. Amen for verbal resolution and a solid takedown. Thank you as well to Deputy Prather who took the time to answer all of my crazy questions.

Thank you to Albert Arnold who took me to the high mountain lakes of Montana for research on horse behavior (and was kind enough to let me out fish him—for once). Your love of nature, horsemanship, and a good laugh are just a few of the things that I respect and love about you.

I would also like to thank Amanda Luedeke who never ceases to amaze. I appreciate your time in working with me to build a ladder which will reach to the stars.

These acknowledgments cannot be finished without sending many thanks to my critique partners Rionna, Casey, Clare, and Pam. You ladies are my best friends. Thank you to Penny and Herb for taking the time to make sure the book 'passes the test.' Thank you all for your open hearts, love, support, and honesty.

And thank you to all of my loyal fans. Your support, love, and kind reviews mean more to me than you can possibly know.

Chapter One

The waves of the lake crashed next to Dane Burke like greedy reporters descending onto a crime scene. Dane picked up the severed hand, careful to touch it only with the tips of his gloved fingers, all in an attempt to save what little evidence remained.

The fingers were wrinkled and pale, the color of rotting fish. The skin of the palm flapped back, exposing the white lines of the tendons and the bloated pink muscles of the victim's hand. He pushed back the skin, covering the hand's viscera. The flesh was rubbed raw in several places, but whether it was from the time in the water or something else Dane couldn't be sure.

Behind him, the secondary officer, Grant, talked with the woman who'd phoned in the find. The woman was blonde, thin, and uncomfortably beautiful.

"So, Aura, are you in Montana for business or pleasure?" Officer Grant asked, with just a little too much glee in his voice.

Dane tried to ignore the amateurish come-ons the officer threw at the blonde with the large blue eyes and plump lips that pulsed with the pink hues of life.

He turned the gruesome hand over in his. The fingernails of the victim were painted a vivid red, now brighter than the blood that had settled in the person's flesh. He snickered quietly as he thought about the stark difference between the woman behind him who was the embodiment of life and the macabre sloughing object of death he stared upon.

Maybe the kid wasn't so wrong for focusing on the woman. If he'd been just a few years younger, maybe he would have been acting that way too—focusing on the beauty of the woman instead of the gore of the job. But he'd long since given up on the things in life that only brought bitterness—death was easier to handle.

Officer Grant mumbled something, and his laughter bounced off the black lake and disappeared into the still of the night. Yet, the woman stayed silent—making Dane like her just a little bit more for avoiding the stupidity that Grant kept unchecked.

This crime scene was going to be one hell of a mess—between the identification and then locking down suspects; the case was going to have to be the focus of his life. He hadn't had a possible homicide for two years. The last case had been cut and dry; man beat his wife, wife murdered husband—mitigated murder. She got two years in prison, a slap on the wrist.

Today all he had was a mutilated hand. Unidentifiable until the DNA came in, no one missing—at least, no one who had been reported missing—and no easy answers. Only one thing seemed likely—there would be a body to follow, but when and if it showed up was a mystery.

Whatever had happened to this woman could only be found in her flesh, unless someone popped up who had witnessed the event. If he had to guess, the hand had been in the water at least a few days. If someone had seen the possible murder, they would turn up soon or not at all.

The skin slipped in his, forcing him to grip it tighter. He laid the evidence down on the bag.

Dealing with suicides and natural deaths was something he did on a regular basis. Yet something about the rotting fish-hand made him shudder. Maybe it was the vibrant party-goer red nail polish and the way it made him think of some of the questionable women he had dated; or it could have been the way it had been removed from the body.

He stood up and wiped off the pebbles from his knees.

"Officer Grant, did you find anything else besides the hand?"

"Excuse me, Ms. Montgarten," the young brown-haired officer said with an overly warm smile.

The woman, Aura, was pretty and all, but the way the kid fawned made him want to gag. The woman was just another person in the long line of crazies they saw each and every day. Polite was fine, but *come on.*

The woman stared down at the hand at Dane's feet.

Officer Grant reached over and touched the woman's arm. "Don't worry about the hand now."

The woman jerked back and away from the boy's touch.

Dane held back the urge to snigger.

She pulled her arms around her body as an icy fall Montana wind blew up off the lake. "Why don't you take her to your car, Officer Grant?" Dane said. "She looks cold."

"No." She glared back at him. "I'm fine."

For a person who'd found the hand floating along the shoreline she seemed oddly quiet. She'd barely spoken since Dane had arrived on scene. Highly suspicious, and if he had to guess, she was the primary suspect. Most people loved to help, to talk away while they explained the crime procedures they had witnessed on *CSI* or some other bullshit television show, but not this woman.

Officer Grant nodded. "I'll grab you a blanket. Deputy Burke is right, you look cold. Can't have you freezing on us."

"I'll just wait in my truck." She spun on her boot's heel and stomped off to her late-model black Dodge towing a white horse trailer.

Officer Grant watched her as she fled from them.

"Grant, you gonna help in the investigation or drool over the blonde all day?"

"Sorry, Deputy. Just wanted to make sure our witness was comfortable."

Comfortable or doable? The kid didn't stand a chance with the woman.

"Did she give you any useable information?"

"Just said she had stopped at the marina and came across the hand."

"Did she say if she saw anyone else around?"

Officer Grant shook his head. "Sounds like there's been no one here but her."

Dane exhaled and watched as his breath made a whirling cloud in the cold air. Of course no one would be around on an evening like this. The lake was too cold, too deep for anyone to be out. "Did she say what she was doing here?"

"Just stopped for a rest."

Stopped for a rest at a marina? There was a campground only ten miles farther down the highway and not much further than that was a line of motels. Signs dotted the roadway advertising the various options to rest. Something didn't add up. "Where's she from?"

"Didn't say."

Rookie…

"Stay here with the evidence. Keep an eye on it. I'm going to go run through some questions with her."

"Sure, Deputy."

From the tone of the kid's voice it was easy to tell he was steadily making another friend in the office. Grant was free to add his name to the ever growing list of people that didn't like Dane Burke. The list was long and distinguished, with several county officials at the top. Dane had never been one to kiss ass or pander to the fickle moods of the politics that ran rampant through this tiny county in the northwest corner of Montana.

The beam of the flashlight bounced over the ground as Dane made his way to the black pickup parked under the lone street lamp. The plates were from Arizona. She was a long way from home.

The woman stared down at a map that lay in her lap as he stepped up to the window. He tapped on the glass with the end of his metal flashlight.

She looked up and shoved the map closed as she rolled down the window. "Officer?" Her cheeks flushed.

"It's Deputy Burke." He pointed to his name badge.

Her overly large eyes sparkled, making him shift uncomfortably in his work boots. "Deputy."

An odd trickle of guilt invaded him. She was suspicious, but he didn't need to be rude—he had worked for his reputation as an even-tempered cop and he didn't need to blow it on one good looking blonde. "Or you can call me Dane. That's my name, Dane Burke."

Great. He mentally groaned. *Now I sound like a freaking idiot.*

"*Dane.*" The corner of her mouth turned up in a little grin. "How can I help you? I think I already answered most of the other deputy's questions."

He pulled a notepad out of his front pocket. "I just have a few more questions for you. Make sure we get all of our bases covered."

She responded with a tight nod.

"Where exactly did you say you were from?"

"I'm just traveling through."

"From Arizona?"

Her blue eyes sparked. "Yeah. Right. Arizona."

So this was how she was going to play it? Like she was some kind of hard ass?

A little dream catcher dangled from her rearview mirror. The blue feather attached to the circle fluttered lazily in the breeze that filtered through the open window.

He clicked his pen and wrote down the word Arizona and her license plate number in a tight scrawl. "Where are you headed to?"

"What does it matter to your case? I told the other officer everything I know. I stopped, found the hand, and I called you guys. That's it. Nothing more."

What was she hiding? He instinctively put on his game face. No emotion, no tells.

"Do you have a horse in the back?" He pointed at the double horse trailer she was towing behind the three-quarter ton.

She glanced down at the side view mirror. "No."

"You moving?" He leaned back and aimed the flashlight at the trailer, but the light was swallowed by the darkness.

"The trailer's empty." Her eyes scanned the mirror again, sparking his inner-cop.

"You mind if I take a look?"

"Do you have a search warrant?"

The woman knew her rights. There was nothing he could do. She may not have had anything to do with the pale, bloated hand that rested on the shore, but there was no question about it, she was hiding something. And even if it killed him, he was going to find out.

Chapter Two

The Diamond Bar Ranch wasn't far from the tiny campground where Aura had spent the night tossing and turning inside the small confines of the horse trailer's tack room. The only thing that had comforted her was the familiar sweet scent of hay and the musky warm scent of horses that permeated the small space.

She stepped up into the cold cab of the truck and took in a long breath. The truck smelled the same as the trailer, but more muted—and still the same scent of safety and of being home.

It was early and the morning sun still slept behind the rugged mountains to her east as she made her way across the tiny town of Somers and north to the turn off to the ranch. The dream catcher bounced on the mirror as she pulled the truck down a long and winding dirt road. The crunch of ice and the smattering of gravel hitting her truck were her only company as she slowly made her way toward the ranch.

Her phone slipped down the dashboard and bumped against the windshield. Aura reached up and took it down. She slid her finger over the screen and opened up the map. She needed to get on the Forest Service lands behind the ranch; it would be the quickest way to get to her sister, Natalie.

Aura poked at her phone with her finger and turned off the screen. She stuffed the phone in her pocket. She was probably fretting over nothing. This wasn't the first time Natalie had gone missing for a few days. Her obnoxiously bohemian life had gotten in the way a few years back, but then it had turned out that she'd been in her horse form for three days with a group of like-minded nymph-shifters and had misplaced her phone.

Her sister was probably off playing wild horse again and had forgotten to charge her phone before she left. Yet, the gnawing in Aura's gut made her think otherwise. Her sister was forgetful, easily distracted, and a bit of a free spirit, but she'd always made it a point to check in when she was out of town.

When she found her, Natalie would be getting a piece of her mind. What had it been, a week now? Seven days from the last time they'd spoken.

When Natalie had left Yuma, it hadn't been on the best of terms. Aura had been busy working with a wild horse, trying to train it for a prima donna who wouldn't let her leave until the horse would do everything from gaiting to a perfect rein. The horse had been a challenge—it had hated the woman as much as she did—but it had eventually responded to Aura's soft touch and gentle intentions.

Natalie had wanted her to come to Montana with her to follow a line on a new job—one that had promised a few thousand dollars that they desperately needed. When things had finally cooled down, Nat had agreed that finishing the job was the best decision and she'd promised to call when she'd gotten to Montana. Yet, she'd only heard from her one time…Seven days ago.

Aura counted her fingers. They'd never gone this long without talking. A sense of dread crept up her spine, but Aura tried to ignore it. Natalie was just being reckless, just taking it for granted that Aura wouldn't worry, thinking she wouldn't fret about her younger sister.

When she did find her, Natalie would undoubtedly make a thousand excuses for why she had gone missing and why she hadn't called.

That was, if she was found.

Aura needed to get through that ranch—whatever it took, she would do it. She unbuttoned the top of her shirt, just low enough that the air from the truck's heater warmed the bare skin on the top of her breasts.

A large arch made of gnarled, skip-peeled logs stood guard over the entrance of the ranch's driveway. The Diamond Bar's brand hung down from the crooked log. The cut steel moved back and forth as an icy wind kicked up, promising of storms that lingered just over the horizon.

Aura tapped nervously on the steering wheel. She pulled around a corner and in the distance she could make out a thickset man standing in the middle of a corral. On the right of the corral was a long building. Its siding was a brilliant red and the windows and door frames were a pristine white, as if the place had recently been painted. Next to the stables sat the big red barn, hay littering the ground in front of the doors.

The man didn't look back as she parked between the barn and the stables and got out. The peal of a horse's scream made chills run through her. What was the man doing?

She rushed around the side of the building as the Quarter Horse's back hooves connected with the metal gate with a clang. The shrill noise made the horse's ears pin back further against its skull. The man bellowed, "Goddamn you! You'll do what I want, you little bastard." There was a slash of a whip through the air and a sharp snap as it connected with the gelding's shoulder, drawing an immediate welt to his sweat-slicked black coat.

The gelding backed up and pressed its rear-end against the metal bars of the corral. The saddle that had been resting on the top of the fence slid off and fell to the ground with a thud. The noise startled the young horse, and he bucked and kicked wildly while the cowboy stood at the center of the ring. The man drew back his whip and slashed it against the gelding's front shoulder.

Anger filled Aura. No horse deserved to be talked to or treated the way the man was treating this horse. All a horse needed to learn was a positive environment and a caring hand. If she didn't do something to help him, this horse would only become more frightened and angry, and that pain and fear would stay in his memory forever—just waiting for a time to be expressed. The horse would only become a time bomb for an incautious rider.

She rushed to the corral. She couldn't do this. She couldn't lose her head. Not now. Not when she needed to find Natalie. She had to make this man an ally, not an enemy. Yet, she had to stop him. The cold fence chilled her fingers as she leaned against the bars.

The crooked-nosed cowboy drew the whip back and smacked it hard against the sensitive tissue on top of the horse's nose, making him scream with pain.

"Stop!" Aura yelled. "Don't hit him again."

The man turned with a start and the horse snorted nervously.

"What the hell are you doing here?" The man spit on the ground.

"I'm looking for the foreman." She couldn't stand looking at the horse—fear and pain filled his eyes. "You shouldn't be hitting that horse. You'll ruin him."

"This ain't no dude ranch."

"Never said it was." She bristled. She had to stay calm.

The man turned toward her and raised his whip as if he intended on striking the strap down upon her fingers.

"Put the whip down, or I will use it on you." The dam cracked inside of her, letting some of the anger stream through.

He lowered the whip as he glared at her from under the brim of his hat. "Goddamn women, think horses need to be baby-handled…"

She tried to bite her tongue. What was wrong with the men in Montana? Did they think just because they lived under the big sky that they didn't have to have manners? That they were above the clouds of civility?

Her boots thumped on the fence as she climbed over and jumped down into the corral. "Let me have that whip."

The man dug his heel into the dirt and his hand clenched around the leather whip. He leaned toward her dangerously, almost as if he considered striking her as he had struck the disobedient horse. "Look, lady, I don't know what the hell you think you're doing here, but you ain't welcome. You can go back over there, climb up into your fancy little truck, and hit the road. I don't need no woman telling me how to handle a horse."

The black Quarter Horse stomped and tapped at the ground nervously with his hoof. The whites of his eyes showed as he bared his teeth. His mouth frothed and sweat rolled down his flanks. He hated the man that stood in the center of the little corral, and it was easy to see why.

She turned to the gelding and stared into his eyes. Men were uncontrollable, but horses, horses she could handle.

For millennia horses had run wild. First the enormous megalithic horses reared across the mountains and plains, commanding respect. As they evolved into the modern horse, humans took them and forced domestication, herding the once regal animals. Some of their wild nature dissipated, bred out and muted by human will.

Men murdered them for meat. Men caged them. They beat them with whips, tied their legs together with rope, and branded them with searing hot irons—anything to beat down their spirits, but whether the horse was Mustang, like her, or like the Quarter Horse standing before her in the corral, they all remained wild at heart. No matter how hard men attempted to enslave and change them, the passion for freedom ran strong in their veins. Throughout time many broke free of their masters and bound across the plains and deserts with only the wind and their will as their guides. They could be beaten, but never was a horse completely broken—instinct would always reign.

The cowboy moved toward the horse, his shoulder straight and rigid, like a sniper going in for the kill. He stepped toward the horse, whip raised.

The Quarter Horse raised its head and eyed the man, the horse's body tensed and his front legs splayed. Controlling fear with more fear was like trying to control the wind by blowing in it. The cowboy was a fool. The horse lunged at the man and the cowboy jumped back to the fence.

"Whoa," Aura whispered to the gelding, putting up her hands and moving between him and the cowboy. The horse drew in a long breath, taking in her scent, and then let out a sharp snort of alarm. His eyes were focused on her. He blinked then nickered with recognition.

"Good boy…"

"His name's Dancer." The man behind her broke the air between her and the horse as he lifted the saddle back onto the fence with a grunt.

The man's movement spooked the horse. Dancer reared back with a furious scream, his front legs in the air.

What had this man done to Dancer before she had arrived? He acted as if he feared for his life. Anger knotted in her gut. That foreman had no business working with horses—there was no reason to hit and cause pain.

"That horse is shit. He's just a hard-headed, resentful bastard. I should've never bought convinced Zeb to buy him at the sale. He shoulda been dog meat."

She looked back over her shoulder toward the man. "The only bastard I see here is you."

"You little—"

"Shut up and let me work."

She turned back to the beautiful black gelding. The muscles on his shoulders twitched. His body was thick and muscular, perfect for strength work, and hungry for action and natural training.

You can trust me, honey. She sent out the thought toward the gelding. Her hands lowered to her sides, her palms up, letting him know that she was open to him. *I won't hurt you.* She stared straight into his eyes.

His head lowered slightly as he stared at her.

"Good boy."

The man chuckled behind her. "You'll never get anywhere by staring."

His voice drove needles over her skin, but she forced her body to relax. This wasn't about the man, this was about the horse.

A drip of froth fell from the horse's mouth and landed on the ground. *It's okay. He won't touch you.* She tried to reassure him. He blinked at her and then lowered his head further. His ear moved forward a tiny bit, still pinned but he was responding to her thoughts.

She kept talking to him, and before long the beautiful black gelding was standing beside her. His head rested on her shoulder.

There was the crunch of gravel and a swirl of dust as a truck drove around the stables and came to a stop next to the corral. Dancer leaned back and his legs shook. She ran her hand down his cheek as she let her relaxed energy flow into him.

A man in shiny camel-colored boots, that were far too clean to have actually seen the everyday work of the ranch, stepped out of the driver side of the pickup. "Who're you?"

She patted Dancer's cheek and urged him to move in a circle around the corral. She turned back to the man as he stopped next to the cowboy with the crooked nose. "I'm Aura."

"Well, Aura, what do you think you are doing with my horse? You have no business touching my livestock."

"I'm saving him."

The man stuffed his thumb in the corner of his jeans pocket and leaned his other arm on the top of the fence. "From what exactly?"

"Your man here," she said, pointing at the crooked-nosed cowboy, "was beating Dancer."

The foreman pushed off from the fence and stared at her like a mad bull. "That's horse shit. I was training that little black devil with the whip, just like I done with every other horse. I ain't beating him. You need to get lost, you little tree hugger."

The rancher put out his hand toward the cowboy, commanding him with a simple motion of his powerful presence. "Stop, Pat. Let the woman talk. I want to hear this." He motioned to her like he could command her as he had done with his employee. "What are you doing here, besides picking a fight with my best hand?"

Everything had gone so wrong. She hadn't intended on picking a fight with Pat, but there were a few things in this world she couldn't stand, and cruelty was one of them. Something like this always brought up the pain from her past and the resentment that had settled within her from hundreds of years of watching idiots with animals.

She didn't stand a chance of getting on the good side of the rancher by going against his crew. The gelding came to a stop beside her and nosed her arm, begging for her to touch him. He nickered softly.

"Look, I wasn't looking for a fight. If your *hand* wouldn't have acted like he didn't have a brain in his head there wouldn't have been a problem." She patted the gelding's soft cheek.

The rancher roared with laughter. "Well, Pat…I guess I can see how this woman pushed you out of your own corral. She's short on words, isn't she?"

Pat's face pulled into a sour pucker and he pushed off from the metal gate. "She didn't push me out."

"I can see that." The rancher dabbed at the corner of his eye with his knuckle.

"I should have pushed his ass in the muck." She pointed down at a steaming pile of manure. "He doesn't deserve to be around a horse."

The rancher's smile faded. "Is that right, miss? You, a stranger who just pulled off the highway, knows more than ol' Pat here? Pat's worked for me for fifteen years. Made some damn fine rodeo horses out of some questionable stock."

She stuffed the toe of her boot into the ground. "Out of fear."

He huffed. "And you think you got a better way, do you, woman?"

The way he said *woman* made the hair on the back of her neck bristle. "I know I got a better way to handle horses." She looked over at Dancer and the horse lifted its head in an agitated sniff, almost as if he was telling her to take the challenge.

Dancer moved his shoulder close to her and nudged her gently. His body was warm as she ran her hands down his length. The muscles on his shoulders quivered with excitement and he motioned his head toward the blanket and saddle. *Not yet, baby. Not yet,* she cooed in her mind. *Let's show them your softer side.*

Aura took a step toward the horse and he moved his flank away, honoring her space. *Good boy.* His ears flicked forward as he listened to her energy. Running her hands down the front of his legs, she tapped his chest. *Lie down, baby.*

Dancer's front end dropped down as he came to his knees, then slowly rolled his body onto his side. His soft underbelly lay exposed, vulnerable.

She knelt down next to the placid horse and ran her hands down his silky black coat. His chest rose and fell in rhythmic motions. "Grab your saddle."

The ranch hand moved toward the saddle, but the rancher stuck out his hand and stopped him. "What did you say your name was, woman?"

"Aura. Aura Montgarten. You?"

"The name's Zeb Burke. I own the Diamond."

"Burke? As in *Dane* Burke?"

The rancher's face went tight and he eyed her suspiciously, his slightly playful demeanor disappeared. "He's my brother. You a friend of his?"

Bringing up the fact that she had met Dane at a crime scene didn't seem like the best idea if she wanted the chance to investigate the land behind the ranch. "We've met."

"And?" He pressed as if he expected her to say she rolled on her back for the man.

"And nothing," she answered, striking down any possible thoughts the man could have about her relationship with Burke.

"You had to think something of him."

She stared at Zeb, trying to find what answer he wanted from the look in his eyes. But he wasn't a horse; she couldn't hear his thoughts or send him hers.

Vague was her best bet to get what she needed.

"I guess he's alright."

"Alright, eh?" His face soured and he motioned toward her truck. "I don't know what my brother told you, lady, but you don't belong here. I don't care what you can do with horses. You need to get off my land."

The ride back to the campsite seemed a lot farther than it had that morning as she chastised herself for her stupid mistake.

At least she'd helped the horse as much as she could—hopefully the jerk, Pat, would let Dancer be. He had great potential if he had only the right training. She forced her mind from the horse.

What was she going to do about Natalie? There was no possibility of her gaining access to the wild lands without getting through that ranch—unless she shifted. And shifting into her Mustang form was out of the question—there were too many people, too many prying eyes, and far too much danger.

There had to be another way.

The road veered to the left and she eased the truck around the bend, where a dirt road connected with the main road.

Instinctively she glanced down the road, looking for traffic. She slammed on the brakes and threw the wheel to the left. A quarter mile down the road a white Ranger sat parked along the side, almost hidden in the overhanging timber.

Aura stopped her truck and got out to inspect the vehicle. A fresh indentation marred the left back panel where red paint streaked the inside of the concave dent. But it was still Natalie's truck.

What was it doing parked there, on the side of an almost deserted back road?

Inside the cab was a black purse, its contents overflowing out onto the seat: lipstick, eyeliner, wallet, keys. The only thing missing was her sister's purple cell phone. Is this where she had parked to access the Forest Service lands? Or had someone else parked the truck here in an attempt to hide it?

The seat was moved all the way back as if someone much taller than her petite sister had been driving. A knot formed in the pit of her stomach. Natalie wasn't the type of girl to let anyone drive her truck.

Aura moved around to the bed of the truck and looked inside. Something caught her eye. Stuffed deep into the front corner of the bed was a white cloth. She reached down and picked up the mysterious cloth. As it unfurled a scream rippled from her throat and echoed out into the still timber.

Chapter Three

Smoke curled up from the embers of the campfire which sat in the middle of the fire pit at the campground. The woman, Aura, must have been there that morning—the ashes were still hot. She couldn't have gone far, but where had she gone? Dane had made it more than clear she wasn't to leave the area until he had gotten a chance to ask her a few more questions.

It wasn't likely she knew anything about the hand, but something inside of him told him there was more to her than met the eye.

He stood up and dusted off his black polyester pants and readjusted the gun that sat on his hip. The little piece of plastic in his ear came to life. "We have report of a trespasser on 19494 Frontage Road, near the Diamond Bar Ranch. Land owner reports seeing a small white female, about twenty-five years old, walking along the fence line…" The dispatcher continued.

There had to be some mistake. A trespasser near Diamond Bar? He walked back to his car and flopped into the driver's seat. There were only four other deputies on today, the closest one was near Creston—too far for him to avoid the assignment. He choked down the bitter taste that filled his mouth as he thought of going near the ranch. He had a job to do. If he was lucky he wouldn't run into anyone from the ranch.

Dane pushed the button on his pager that connected him to dispatch. "Two-nine-seven, two-six-five. I'll take the call."

Who would be so stupid to trespass around the ranch? Everyone that lived in the area lived by a strict code of ethics—a "you got my back and I got yours" mentality. If the cattle broke loose and onto the road, the neighbors would be out there to help in a moment's notice. It was the one thing that kept everyone working and safe in the long, harsh Montana winters and hot, dust-filled, and monotonous summers.

He pulled the car onto the highway with a smattering of gravel and raced toward the ranch. With any amount of luck at all he could take care of this call with a little verbal resolution—in and out, simple.

The wheel automatically turned down the road that had led to his home for two decades, but now took him to a place he didn't belong. His hand gripped the wheel so hard his fingers tingled.

Just short of the ranch's long driveway sat the little white house that matched the address the dispatcher had given him. The petite woman had wispy, silvery hair that sat high on her head and bobbed like a little hat as she waved him down. He had known the woman, like most of the year-round residents, his entire life. His lips cracked as he forced a smile.

The woman made her way to the driver's side window as he pulled to a stop.

"Little Danish, I was hoping you would be the one I got. I heard about the hand. I hope they find whoever it belonged to. Nasty bit of business if you ask me."

He cringed as she said his childhood nickname. She was lucky she was pushing eighty or he would have had to remind her that he was almost thirty and nowhere near the appropriate age to be called "little Danish."

Dane forced a smile. "It's nice to see you, Mrs. Mullen. Can you tell me about the woman you saw?"

"I'm telling you, this is just strange. There was a little lady out here this morning walking down the fence line. It was about 7:30. I think she was thinking she could get away without being noticed. But she didn't know this lady." Mrs. Mullen pointed at her chest proudly. "There ain't no way I'm gonna let the day pass me by. I had bread to bake this morning."

The woman continued babbling as Dane pretended to listen about the details of her morning and what she thought the young woman was up to.

"Which way did she go?"

"I watched her for a while. She was headed toward the back forty of the Diamond. Ain't nothing back there but a few horses."

The chatter continued until he could politely pull away from the woman and head down the fence line and away from the assault to his ears. Surely by the end of the day the news of a trespasser would be circulating around Somers and he would be fielding calls and texts from people wondering what was going on.

There was a thin layer of crispy white frost on the grass and the barbed wire which stretched up the hill as far as he could see. After a couple of miles, he came over the crest of a pine-covered hill. A bare patch of barbed wire caught his attention where the woman must have gone through the fence. Of course he had put on his nice work shoes this morning; his feet would be soaked almost as soon as he stepped into the ranch's deep grass. The call was getting better and better as the minutes ticked by. Not only did he have to be on the ranch, he had to do it without seeing his brother; if he didn't get shot at, he would have to consider himself lucky.

The wire creaked as he pushed through it, careful not to get his uniform stuck on the rusty barbs. A head stuck up from over the ridge line. Instinctively, he reached for his gun.

"Stop!"

The blonde head disappeared before he could get a good look at her face.

Dane's footfalls were muted by the thick grass as he rushed up the hill. He tried to control his breath as he pushed his legs up the steep ascent. The woman's long hair flowed behind her as she sprinted down the ravine toward a dry creek bed. "I said stop!"

His voice echoed off the empty hillsides and down toward the woman.

• • •

How had Deputy Burke found her?

An animalistic instinct to run, to get away from the man chasing her, poured through Aura like liquid flames. Aura's human feet caught in the long, frost-covered grass as she tore her way toward the end of the ridge. If she could just get down to the bottom, then slip around the bend of the hill, she could get away.

If she could just get away, she wouldn't have to answer any more questions or tell him about the macabre find she'd made in the back of Natalie's pickup. She was already likely a suspect from the wayward hand—the last thing she needed to do was tell the police that she'd found a bloody camisole in her sister's deserted pickup. They'd lock her away in a second and she didn't have time to waste playing some small town cop's stupid game.

The thought to shift into her palomino form passed through her mind, but she pushed it away. He couldn't see what or who she was. He would never stop chasing her—it had happened before and it could never happen again. She was safer as a human, regardless of what Natalie thought. A horse was far more vulnerable.

She turned and glanced back over her shoulder at the muscular man. His jaw was set like it had been forged in iron. His hand was at his hip, gun at the ready. "Aura Montgarten, I said stop!"

The crash of his feet followed her down the hillside. He wouldn't shoot her, would he? Over the decades so much had changed, but the new law wouldn't allow for him to shoot her, would it? She picked up speed. Let him shoot. There was only one way to kill her and if he never got close, he would never get the chance.

"If you don't stop, I will be forced to taze you!"

The sounds of his heavy breaths grew closer. He knew who she was. She had nowhere to run. She had to find Natalie, and she would stay in Somers until she did, so fighting with the local law enforcement didn't seem like the smartest move.

Her feet refused to stop, but her mind forced them to slow.

There was a footstep behind her. His arm wrapped around her waist and his shoulder drove into the middle of her back, throwing her off balance. Her face smacked against the cold wet grass and her mouth filled with dirt as his body pinned her to the ground. Before she could stop him, he had her arms pulled behind her back.

She thrashed on the ground, fighting the sexy predator. His face was close to hers and the minty scent of his breath mixed with the masculine spice of his cologne.

It surprised her, but beneath her need to escape something else welled within her, something more primal, more voracious—was it desire? Was it a need for him to push her down in another way? How would it have felt if he was coming after her to make love? To press her against the ground and steal the kisses from her wanting lips?

"What the hell do you think you are doing?" Dane growled.

Aura pulled at her arms, trying to pull them free from his vise-like grip, but his fingers refused to budge. He sat up on top of her, his muscular thighs wrapped around her middle. The heat of his body crept into the chilled skin of her back, making the desire that nibbled at her grow more ravenous.

She turned so she could see him. His face had the same forged look. His eyes drilled into her with an adrenaline-laced fury; as if she was a beast he was hell-bent on destroying. With the strength of his features and the ferocity of his gaze she was under his control and a strange need sprang up from her core. She liked this. She liked his body pressing against hers, holding her down, and for a moment, controlling her. She couldn't feel this way. Not about this man or any man. Not now. Not here. No one could control her.

"Why in the hell did you run?"

The course dirt at the corner of her lips fell into her mouth as she moved to talk. "Why did you chase me?"

Dane sat back a little, shifting his weight from her back to her ass. "I'm trained to run."

Well, so am I...

"You were reported for trespassing on the Diamond Bar Ranch. Are you aware that what you are doing is against the law?"

She had seen the red *No Trespassing* signs, but admission was tantamount to guilt. She wasn't about to be sent to jail for some stupid law—not when her sister's life could be at stake.

"Get off of me," she grunted.

"You gonna run?"

The muscles of Aura's legs tensed as she thought about running, but she shook her head. She couldn't act like a fool. If she went to jail there would be no one to help Natalie.

Dane's fingers uncurled from her wrist and her arms freed. She wiggled and Dane sat up, slightly allowing her just enough room to roll over and face him.

The anger in his eyes melted away as he looked down at her. The warmth of his body seeped into her like a warm cup of tea after a long day, and she basked in his inadvertently calming touch. Without thinking, her hands dropped to the tops of his thighs. A spark jumped between them, through the thin cloth of his pants and through her body, straight to her heart. His eyes softened and his body relaxed under her touch.

He seemed to shake his head slightly as if he was fighting the voices in his head. "What were you doing here, Aura?"

Something about the way he looked at her, like she was the woman in his life instead of a stranger pinned beneath the legs of an officer, made her want to tell him the truth—that she was in

Somers to find her sister. She didn't want to be alone in carrying the weight of Natalie's disappearance anymore. Maybe Dane could be just the man to help her.

"I need to get back into the timber." She thought about the shirt that she had stuffed in her back pocket, but hesitated in telling him anything about her sister. She was already likely under arrest for trespassing; things would only grow worse if she showed him the blood-covered shirt.

"You were going to trespass through the ranch to get back into the timber?" His hands dropped to hers and he had a confused expression on his face. "Why?"

"I needed a good run."

"You needed a run? Through a ranch you have no business being on—alone?"

"No." She turned her palms up to him, letting him run his rough thumb over her sensitive skin. Her heart raced with excitement. "Now I have you to help me get onto Shirley Mountain." She jerked her head in the direction of the mountain that sat to her left.

"Have *me*?" He flashed a wicked smile. "You think I'm going to hang out with some drifter who thinks she can trespass where she wants, whenever she wants?"

In a moment of shear madness, she pulled her hands from his, reached up, grasped his black uniform, and pulled him down to her. He didn't resist. His mouth tasted like peppermint as she pulled his lip into the edge of her mouth and sucked. A quiet needy moan rumbled from his chest as their kiss deepened.

He pushed his hand up behind her ear and ran his thumb over the skin of her cheek, stroking the need she felt for him. She wanted this. Him. Here. Now.

"You'll help me. Won't you?" She let her nymph magic go to work as the sweet seduction dripped from her words.

His other hand moved between her shoulders, never stopping their hungry kiss.

"Whatever you need. I'm yours. I promise," he replied, his voice hazy with her spell.

The man's full lips moved with hers, his tongue flicked against hers making the dampness grow between her thighs. He let go of her face and grabbed her hand and pushed it up over her head, into the moist grass.

He pulled back slightly, but his lips still touched hers. "You're so fucking sexy."

His words filled her with an unbridled excitement and she took his lips hard, like a wildfire overtaking virgin timber. Many men had wanted her, but Dane was so much more than most—he was a predator and she the prey, the hunter and she the hunted.

Icy winds picked up around them, forcing their bodies closer together. She ran her fingers around the top of his belt and slowly unclipped his gun. Her right hand slid up under his shirt, covering the motion of her left. He moaned as her fingers caressed the firm muscles of his core. *Was he this muscular everywhere?*

Her mouth pressed against his and she raised her hips against his responding body. The gun steadily moved from the holster as she pulled. She slipped it free and slid the cold steel under her back.

She reached back up and unbuttoned his uniform top and pulled it from his shoulders, uncovering the white tee-shirt he wore beneath. The muscles of his chest pressed hard against his shirt, showing every perfect line and contour of his work-strengthened body. She dropped the black shirt with the badge pinned to it to the ground beside them. A sense of guilt filled her as she thought of what she had done, but she needed to protect herself.

Dane pushed her legs apart and rubbed his heat against her. The moan rippled from her lips. His hand found the hem of her shirt and he reached underneath. His rough fingers pulled down the cup of her bra and he thumbed her sensitive nipple. She lifted her hips to meet him as her need to possess him burned through.

He slid his body against hers, showing her exactly how much he needed her in return.

Pulling in a raspy breath, he drove his face down against her neck. She moaned as he passed his body over hers again.

The grass rustled above them and there was a clatter of hooves on rock.

Dane sat up. Above them, on the ridgeline, was the ranch hand, Pat. He sat high in the saddle of a bay-colored horse. He leaned back and the leather of the saddle creaked.

A part of Aura was glad to see the surly cowboy—what had she been thinking in seducing Dane?

She pushed him off. He grabbed his shirt and threw it on over his tee-shirt as he tried to cover up the evidence of the mistake Aura had made.

"Goddamn it." Dane reached down to his belt. "Where's my goddamn gun?"

"Old Mrs. Mullen told me there was a trespasser." Pat shifted in the saddle as he pitched his head back in a laugh. Aura noticed a bulge on Pat's hip, similar in shape to the gun that rested under her back. "I guess this must be the new way you all are arresting law-breakers. I guess I can see why murder is on the rise."

Chapter Four

What in the hell was he thinking? How had he allowed her to do that to him? It was like Dane was under some kind of spell. One minute he was arresting her and the next...well, the next he was making a goddamned fool of himself. And in front of Pat no less. *Son of a bitch.*

It was because of those eyes, those big sapphire-colored eyes. All she'd had to do was flash them at him, flick her little eyelashes, and he had been a goner. Not in the last five years had he experienced anything like what she had done to him in that field. Hell, he couldn't remember a time a woman had made him lose his mind like that.

Dane slammed his hand against the steering wheel of the patrol car. The worst part of it all was that he'd loved every goddamned second of it—being in her arms, her pulling him down to her, feeling her writhe beneath him as he kissed her.

"You didn't need to handcuff me," Aura growled from behind the clear plastic barrier window.

"You didn't need to touch my gun." He opened the door to the patrol car, stepped out, and slammed it shut without waiting for her to respond. She'd already gotten him into enough trouble without bringing him into a verbal conflict.

She threw her head against the back seat in agitation. Dane reached down and checked his holster. His gun was still there.

The white ranch house where he'd grown up sat at the end of a long path of flat, sharp black stones covered in the leafy debris of the early fall. Planters filled with frostbitten flowers lined the path. The wraparound porch was empty except for a single chair where Zeb sat with his booted foot resting on his knee and a smug grin on his face.

Dane pulled the little notebook out of his pocket. This was just another call. His feet seemed to stick in place, like he'd stepped in a steaming hot pile of cow manure. The last time he'd seen Zeb had been the day he'd left this place and vowed he'd never come back. Fate had a wicked sense of humor. That's what he got for saying "never."

The boot-worn steps creaked as he stepped up and onto the porch. Zeb rocked slightly in his chair as he stared intently at Dane. Dane stared right back. His brother wasn't going to take control of this situation like he tried to take control of everything else. Dane was the cop here, he was the authority. Zeb could respect it, or he could kiss his ass.

Zeb dropped his boot to the deck with a thud. "Hey, you got a little something right there." He leaned forward toward him and pointed at his lip.

Dane ran his finger over the edge of his lip. On his fingers was the smear of a faint pink lipstick. He rubbed his fingers together angrily until the stain disappeared.

"Mr. Burke, did you wish to press charges against this woman?" He jabbed his finger toward the car.

His brother leaned back in the rocking chair and put his hands down on the armrests. "What was she doing here? Going after my horses again?"

She'd been here before? Funny how she'd forgotten to mention it to him. Come to think of it, she'd not said anything about why she'd been on the property.

"You and I both know that there aren't any horses back in that pasture." He opened the pad of paper and lifted a pen from his front pocket. "Charges? Yes or no."

Zeb peered out to the car. "She's pretty, isn't she?"

Dane's gut clenched and bile rose, burning his throat as he swallowed it down. "If you don't tell me yes, I'm going to assume you are passing on your right to pursue legal recourse."

"Tell her she has an open invitation to dinner." Zeb gave a little wave in the direction of the patrol car.

Dane flipped the pad closed and stuffed the pen in his pocket. His brother would never change.

• • •

The air was humid and stale from her breath as it filled the little plastic confine of the patrol car's back seat. Her butt was sore from sitting in the same place for so long and she shifted in the seat.

Dane's brows were furrowed in an angry pucker. He could write her the ticket. She didn't care. So she'd trespassed on the ranch. She had bigger things to worry about.

He got in the car and slammed the door shut. The car hummed to life. He spun it around and made his way to the icy road. The only sound was the crackle and sputtering of the patrol car's radio.

The car bumped to a stop at the edge of the highway. "You need to tell me the truth." Dane swiveled in his seat to face her. "What were you doing on that ranch?"

"Going for a hike."

He turned around, threw the transmission into park, and turned back. "Look, you can give me more of your bullshit or you can answer me. Tell me the truth and I won't have to lock you up."

She cringed as she thought about sitting behind bars. If she was locked up there would be no one who'd be able to help Natalie. No one, other than her, cared or would know where to look. Aura let her gaze settle on the handsome man that stared at her. It would be nice to have a powerful ally, and Dane Burke wasn't hard to look at...or hard to kiss.

"I don't do well in a confined space. Let me out and I will tell you everything. My truck's a mile back. When I'm done, you have to promise to let me go."

"Go where?"

Did he not want her to leave? No. He must see her like any other criminal, she was just another form to fill out, another report to write.

"I'll stay around Somers as long as I need to. When I get what I came for then I'm leaving—and that's the God's honest truth."

He turned to the front and put his hands on the wheel and tapped his fingers, as if he was thinking about really letting her go. After a moment he got out and opened her door.

Dane stared down at her through the open door. "If I do this, you have to stay here until all of my questions are answered. No running off, or I will put a warrant out for your arrest. Got it?"

She slid to the edge of the seat and stuck her legs out the door. "I got it."

Her hand grazed the rough fabric of his uniform, and the lust she had felt when he'd pinned her down to the ground filled her once again. Damn her nymph urges. Why couldn't she control this lust that she felt around Dane? It was normally not a problem. She'd been alive long enough that it was usually easy to turn on and off the switch between her seductive nymph-like being and simple, albeit beautiful, pseudo-human, but not around the handsome brunette who'd lain between her thighs.

Their eyes connected for a split-second, allowing her to enjoy the faint gold sparkles in the warm brown of his irises. Her heart fluttered like a hummingbird's as his lips quivered into a sexy melting half grin. A faint warmth rose up her neck and spread to her face. She quickly dropped her gaze to the ground, breaking the connection.

The gravel crunched under him as he turned away from her and let her step out of the car.

"Are you going to tell me what you were doing at the ranch or what?"

His pants pulled against the round muscles of his ass as he walked a few steps away. If she was going to work with anyone, she could definitely work with this chiseled specimen of human man.

Besides, he didn't need the whole truth. And perhaps he could fill in a few of the blanks. He had access to resources she could only hope for.

Dane spun around and pointed at her assertively. "Listen…I don't know what the hell came over me back there." He motioned in the direction of the ranch with his head. "But it doesn't change the fact that you broke the law."

Her gut wrenched. She had started to seduce him, admittedly, but he couldn't turn her away. No man was able to refuse her, not once they tasted the forbidden fruit that was her kiss.

"You're beautiful…I mean really goddamned beautiful. But I have a job to do. I can't let you or anything else, get in the way."

So he didn't want her then? *Even better.* No sexual relationship would be necessary and she could use him to help her find Natalie. *Not that the sex would be bad.*

Aura glanced over at the deputy. He was right. He had a job to do, but so did she.

"I understand." She stood up and slammed the car door shut behind her. He wouldn't be putting her back in that place. Ever. "You and I…It was a mistake. It's just not every day I get swept off my feet by a man in uniform."

"You call getting apprehended 'getting swept off your feet'?" He smiled and his teeth shone brightly in the morning sun. "I'd hate to think what would happen if I was really trying."

So would she.

"I haven't had a lot of great experiences in my life." She leaned back against the patrol car, careful to keep her gaze firmly planted on the tips of her boots.

"I hope that someday that can change for you." The tension buzzed between them for a moment. "Does the ranch have anything to do with these experiences?"

It struck her as strange that this man would ask such a personal question, but then she reminded herself that he was an officer of the law. It was his job to ask the real questions, the questions that most people danced around.

"Not the ranch exactly. It's only a speed bump."

Dane pushed his arms over his chest and his face moved into the practiced stoic face of a seasoned officer. "What does that mean?"

"I need to get to Shirley Mountain and the Forest Service land behind the ranch." She stopped there, hoping he would simply say he had a way. She silently begged that she wouldn't have to expose herself any more than she already had to this man. "And I need your help."

"What's there? Behind it? What are you looking for?"

Of course he would continue to press her for answers. Damn cops.

She bit the edge of her lip until the faint taste of blood filled her mouth. "My sister, Natalie, is missing."

There was barely a flicker on Dane's face. "Did you file a missing persons report?"

He was always about work. Of course Natalie was just like any other girl who had gone missing. He couldn't possibly realize how much more she was, nymph, friend, and sister. Natalie was her everything.

"She's been missing seven days now. The last time I talked to her she was somewhere close to Somers. Her phone was traced back to that stretch of land." She pointed at the sprawling mountains that rose up so tall their blue tips tore at the underbellies of the clouds that tried to pass over.

"How do you know she's missing and not just failing to call you?"

"We talk every day." Irritation poured out of her voice and she instantly felt guilty. He didn't know. He was only doing his job.

"So she wasn't angry with you?"

"Yes, but not enough to stop calling. I just couldn't make it to Montana with her—I had to finish with a client—she got mad, but she's not the type to hold a grudge for something that asinine."

"What kind of client?" He gave her a sideways glance.

"I'm a horse trainer."

He nodded approvingly, but something about him still made it seem like her every move was being scrutinized. "You're from Arizona, correct?"

She glared at him. "You know the answer to that. I'm sure you did your little background check."

He looked away from her. "Why was Natalie in Somers?"

Aura held back the desire to give him a snippy reply. He was trying to help. "She'd gotten a line on a great job from a friend. When she got up here, the job had dried up, but she liked it so much her friend convinced her to stay. They were hiking, then she just up and disappeared."

Dane pulled the pad of paper from his pocket. "What makes you assume there has been any foul play?"

"She'd told me she'd been staying with a friend not far from the marina."

"Was that what you were really doing there? Looking for evidence of your sister?"

She answered with a short nod. "I need you to make me a promise...I'll tell you everything you need to know on one condition."

"And what is that?"

"I want to be involved in every aspect of this case."

"Impossible. I'm a cop. You're a civilian. Have you ever heard of boundaries?"

"Boundaries are made to be broken…" She smiled. "Now do you want to help me find Natalie or not?"

Dane shook his head resignedly. "I can't promise you'll be included with everything, but I will let you be as involved as I can."

"Fair," she said excitedly.

His eyebrows shot up. "So, if you're telling the truth now, what do you really know about the hand we found at the marina?"

Of course he would think she had something to do with the hand. "All I know is that it wasn't hers. My sister would never wear red nail polish. She's too much of an *artist*." Aura reached into her back pocket and pulled out the bunch of cloth she stuffed in it before she'd left. "Which means she wouldn't have had any need for this." She lifted up the blood smattered camisole with lace around its edges. "I found it in the back of her deserted truck."

"What the hell?" He took the cloth and inspected it, then looked up at her. "You do realize that you've destroyed whatever evidence we could get from this? And why didn't you tell me you found her truck? You do know what this could mean don't you?"

Was he really going to lecture her?

"Why didn't you tell me about this before you trespassed on the Diamond?" He jabbed the shirt at her.

"I called you about the hand—and look where that landed me." *Right into the lap of the one man I should be running from.* "And besides, that's not Natalie's shirt. She doesn't wear that kind of stuff. And I'm only here to find her."

He twisted it gently around as he inspected the fabric. "Maybe we can still get a DNA sample from some of the blood."

"I already told you, it's not her shirt."

"Well, whoever's shirt this is, there's a good chance that they aren't alive." He lifted it up so she could see the thin small hole that pierced the fabric of the front, just over where the wearer's heart would have been. The dried brown blood ran around the hole and down the front of the shirt.

Dane was right. Someone out there, someone who was somehow involved with her sister, lay dead.

Chapter Five

Just another great day at the office. Dane pulled the evidence bag shut around the white camisole. The lights of the patrol cars reflected against the snow as it blanketed the ground around the white Ranger.

He couldn't wrap his mind around the fact that Aura hadn't called the police when she'd found the bloody top. Who in their right mind would take evidence from a crime scene and stuff it in their pocket? The only thing he could fall back on was that she had been afraid to call the police about her sister's disappearance. But why? What was she hiding?

The sergeant tracked through the thin layer of fresh snow toward him. "We've collected some hair samples and we found a small amount of blood pooled in the bed of the truck. We will send them off to the crime lab and see what we can get."

Dane handed the man the bag with the shirt inside. "I'm hoping they can pull some DNA from this. I don't know how much use it will be, but maybe we can get something."

What had Aura's sister gotten into? Was she the murderer or was she going to turn up as another victim? For now, he could only hope that Natalie was still alive.

He glanced over at Aura. Her arms were pulled tight across her chest and she stared out in the direction of the timber that grew tall and dark along the sides of the logging road. If she hadn't gotten turned around coming out of that ranch, she would have never run across the crime scene. She was either the luckiest or the least lucky woman he'd ever met—she kept popping up in the worst places for her and the best places for him to get a handle on the sudden wave of crime that was hitting the county.

What did all these crimes have to do to with her and her sister? Something about it all sat in him like a soured turkey sandwich. There was just something so wrong. If he didn't get to the bottom of it soon, there would be hell to pay—not only within the department and the people of Flathead County, but within him as well. He couldn't let a woman die in his county and let the murderer get away with it. Not to mention a possible missing person case.

Aura chewed on her lip like an angst-filled mother. A strange sense of guilt and empathy roiled in his stomach. He tried to swallow it away. *She's just another face, another name in the books—even if I did kiss her, even if she is sexy as hell, I can't think of her like anything more. I'll lose my objectivity and my reputation.*

No matter how hard he tried to rid himself of the feelings, they remained.

One of the secondary officers pushed out from the pine boughs and stepped up onto the road. "Sarge? I think we got something down there." He pointed down the hill in the direction he'd come. "I think I found our vic."

Aura's face blanched and her arms tightened. He stepped toward her. A profound need to hold her flooded his senses. She needed him. She was strong, but she looked so terrified.

He stopped just short of her, and held his arms to his sides. "You stay here. We can't have you contaminating another crime scene."

She nodded.

Dane turned and made his way to the road's edge. The officer led the way down the steep, slippery hill. He worked back and forth through the underbrush like a well-trained bloodhound. The sergeant walked ahead of him, grunting as he stepped over downed logs and tripped on the tiny bushes that littered the ground.

The pit in his stomach grew. Every part of him hoped that the person the officer had found wouldn't be Natalie. Aura would be devastated. She cared so much for her sister. It was easy to see that her life revolved around finding the woman, and if she had been murdered …

The man led them to the edge of a wide pit where a pine had fallen, pulling its roots out of the ground. Its root ball stuck up from the far side of the pit, the top of it covered in a layer of snow. Dane stopped and stared down into the natural grave. At the bottom lay a dark-haired woman. She lay face down in the dirt. An icy breeze slid by him and slipped down into the hole, pushed the listless brown hair from the woman's neck, and exposed the black horse tattooed on the base of her cervical vertebrae.

What was his ex-wife Angela doing here? Dane's breath caught in his throat. *Zeb was going to have a holy shit fit when he learned they'd found his wife dead.*

Dark ruby red trails of dried blood clung to her neck like feasting worms.

Dane fell to his knees.

• • •

The hillside was slick as Aura worked her way down to Dane. He'd told her to stay behind, but the need to know for sure gnawed at her. If the victim was Natalie…well, it couldn't be Natalie—but if it was, someone was going to pay.

Her foot slipped on an icy patch and she grabbed a handful of pine tree to stop herself from falling. Her heart thrashed in her chest as she regained her footing. Something wrapped around her fingers as she tried to pull them from the sapling. Aura glanced at her hand. Around her fingers was a handful of long black horse hair.

The hair was darker than Natalie's. Aura lifted it to her nose and sniffed. The uric scent was strong, full of hormones, and there was a faint hint of something else that she couldn't identify. From the urea it had to be a hair from another Mustang-shifter, but who?

The rumble of the sergeant's voice broke her concentration. She wrapped the hairs in a Kleenex and stuffed the little square into her pocket. Dane would be pissed that she was concealing evidence, but she couldn't risk exposing her kind. He wouldn't learn anything even if he followed the horse lead.

Natalie had come here on the promise of a job at a ranch, but had there been another reason that she had been lured to this place? Had Natalie been hiding the truth from her in the same way Aura was hiding the truth from Dane?

Standing on the edge of a wide pit was the stiff-backed sergeant; at his side were Dane and another officer who clicked away with a digital camera. Dane was crouched in a tight ball, almost like a tiger waiting to strike. Aura's hands shook as she made her way to them. Nausea rolled through her as the cold putrid scent of death wafted up from the pit.

Dane stood up. "Don't come any closer."

She pushed past him and peered in. There was a brunette woman at the bottom she didn't recognize.

The woman's left hand was missing.

A sense of pity for the woman passed through her, quickly followed by relief. The nausea disappeared.

Natalie is still alive.

"Thank the gods."

"What?" Dane stared at her with a pinched angry look upon his face. "What the hell do you mean by that? You're happy my ex-wife is at the bottom of a pit?"

The wavering nausea returned and she covered her mouth as she stared at the black tattoo that matched her own. She reached back and ran her fingers over her skin, trying to hide their shared secret. It was so hard to kill a nymph—who ever had killed the woman must have known the truth of their existence. No bullet, no drowning, nothing could kill them. The murderer was either aware of their secret, or the murderer was a nymph...like Natalie.

"I'm sorry." *Dane had been married to a horse-shifter. Did he know about her kind?* "I...I didn't realize."

He looked back toward the pit and away from her apologetic gaze, but there was no sign he knew the truth about her or her kind.

"Goddamn it." His shoulders fell and there was an air of vulnerability that surrounded him. "Who would want to kill her? She was no saint, but why?"

"I'm so sorry," she said almost in a whisper. Before she could stop herself, Aura leaned down and wrapped her arms around his back and pressed her face into the sweet scent of his neck like he was one of her injured horses—another soul in need of help.

He reached up and touched her hand that rested below his chin. "You didn't know."

No...but she hadn't known that he'd been married before either. The revelation came as such a surprise; Dane hadn't seemed like the type that would get a divorce. He seemed strong, centered, and devoted. What had happened that would have driven him to leaving his wife? Or had she left him because she was a shifter? Had she wanted to protect him from the curse of their kind? Her leaving would make sense of the way he was one minute so close and in the next forcing himself away. She must have hurt him almost beyond repair.

His hand slipped from hers and he tensed beneath her arms. She was suddenly all too aware that she had committed a faux pas in front of Dane's sergeant and fellow officer. What had she been thinking? She had made Dane look weak in front of his comrades.

"I'm sorry for your loss." She released her hands and stepped away from him.

"Thanks." Dane's face was turned from her as he nodded. He gave a long sigh, as if he was trying to express his sadness and anger in the only way he could.

The sergeant gave her an appreciative nod, as if he was relieved that the quick display of emotion had come to a stop. His world must have been such a drain it was no wonder he avoided emotions—dealing with death and mayhem each day must take a heavy toll on the men of the force.

She had so many questions. What did this woman have to do with her sister? And why would they find her body so close to the truck? Did Natalie have something to do with this woman's death?

The sergeant clicked on his radio and notified dispatch of the body in a low, brusque, monotone voice. The flash of the other officer's camera bounced off the snow, illuminating the dark shadows that rested around the body.

For the second time in as many days, Aura felt horribly out of place, like a demon in a church choir. The radio's static filled the forest, echoing the emotions that buzzed within her.

Why had she allowed herself to become involved with the police? Why did she have to be so close to her enemy? Especially a man who was secretive, work-obsessed, and so handsome that every time she was near she wanted to press her body against him and bask in his strong manly scent like a puppy nuzzling its master.

Aura tried to relax and let the emotions cascade from her, but a creeping sensation swept up and down her spine.

A long shaft of sunlight pierced the clouds above them and shone down on crisp a patch of fresh snow about fifty yards away. A white snowshoe hare sat in the snow staring at them, the only thing moving was the thin little whiskers around its triangular, flat nose. The black-tipped ears froze as it stared at her with its perfectly round eyes as if it waited for her to move, to attack.

The same energy that had filled her when she'd been near the horse tickled her senses. The hare stared at her. The little animal was scared.

The wind picked up and the rabbit's gaze flashed to the right where a tall mound of dirt sat half covered in brush. Something on the hillside to its right was disturbing him. Her heartbeat echoed the creature's, fast and erratic, ready for danger. She tried to keep the energy between them flowing, but with such a small animal it was a challenge. She couldn't make out what the animal was afraid of; it was something large, uncommon, and more importantly, unwelcome in the mammal's territory.

Dane stood up and stepped back, breaking a stick with a loud snap. Before she could urge the hare to stop, it had zigzagged away from the danger of Dane and whatever was to the right of the tall mound of dirt.

Aura tried to seem unhurried as she picked her way through the strangling limbs of the brush to where the hare had sat. The animal's tracks were long oval shapes in the snow, followed by long skiffs where it had made its dashing getaway. Behind the snowy mound something blue caught her eye.

She stepped nearer to the blue object, to get a closer look. It had crisscrossed lines across its surface. She reached out to touch the shiny plastic.

"What are you doing?" Dane said, surprising her.

"Nothing." She stopped and pointed her finger at the object. "I think I might have found something. Come check this out."

His footsteps crunched in the snow as he made his way next to her. "What the hell?" He slipped a pair of black leather gloves on and stepped toward the blue plastic. He stopped and looked back to her. "I think it's a tarp."

"Hey, Grant?" he yelled. "You done with that camera?"

Officer Grant meandered in their direction. "Coming."

The officer clicked away behind them taking photos as Dane pulled up the edge of the tarp. It crackled as its frozen surface begged to be left untouched. He pulled in a harsh breath and then slowly exhaled, his breath making a swirling white cloud.

Under the tarp was a mass of dark brown hair attached to the pale skin of a young woman. She was probably in her early twenties and her mouth was open, as if she had been screaming when she'd died.

"Is this your sister?" Dane motioned to the woman with a jab of his thumb.

Aura couldn't take her eyes away from the white skin of the woman. She was so pale. Her lips were drained of blood and were only a slight shade darker than her ghostly flesh. What had happened to these women?

"Aura?"

She jerked at the sound of her name. "No…It's not her." The relief that she had been feeling slipped into a sense of foreboding—the chances were slipping away that Natalie was still alive. "I need to get out of here. I can't stand this anymore."

Dane's gaze snapped to her. "I'm sorry. I should have realized… you shouldn't be here."

The snow squeaked as she spun on her heel, away from the woman's frozen gaze. She stepped up the hill and her foot slipped. Beneath her foot was an ice-covered purple rectangle.

"Dane…" She gasped. Her finger shook as she pointed at the familiar object. "Look."

Dane sprinted over as quickly as the slick snow would allow. Aura pointed at the little purple rectangle that lay exposed.

"Grant, you need to take a few more pictures for evidence," Dane ordered.

The secondary officer slipped as he walked over and took several quick photos. As he finished, Dane leaned down and picked up the tiny cell phone from the snow with the edge of a plastic bag. "Maybe we can dry it out. Get some information from it. Figure out who the phone belonged to and who they called." He sounded like a kid who'd just found the decoder ring at the bottom of a cereal box.

His excitement made the fist of nerves in her stomach clench, pushing the bile up into her throat. She swallowed it down like a poisonous draught as she attempted to find her voice. The acid burned at her throat, threatening to close down the little faculty for speech that she could still muster. "You don't need it to work… It's Natalie's…The thing died when…when I was talking to her."

"Are you sure?"

Aura reached down and lifted the bag from Dane's pinched fingers. Her hope pulsed through her, maybe she was wrong. Maybe she was being a little too jumpy. It was possible the cell could belong to one of the icy corpses. She closed her eyes as she silently mouthed a prayer to the gods.

She'd never been one for prayer, for silly hopes, and least of all for bohemian art—unlike Natalie. She'd loved the stuff. The more ethereal, the more out-there, the more her sister had loved it. The love went so far to even include her phone. One day, Aura had walked in to find Natalie painting over-simplified, gaudy pink flowers on the front edges of her purple phone. If there was any one who loved Aura up in the heavens, they would do her this one solid favor and there would be no awful pink flowers on this phone.

The wet phone slid down in the bag like a thousand pound weight. It jerked and twisted, mimicking the slow rhythmic slide of blood as it oozed to her core, protecting her from the potential freezing pain of finding more of her sister's evidence— and confirming that there was less of a chance that she was still alive. The thud of the phone hitting the bottom hit her with the emotional weight of a freight train.

The bag turned as if in slow motion. A bit of heavy snow thumped to the ground a few yards away. From the corner of her eye, Dane's breath formed an arcing cloud. In the distance, the low rumble of the sergeant's voice echoed up off the snow.

The plastic bag crinkled as she looked down at the face of the phone.

In that moment, those damned pink flowers, with their malformed edges, incinerated the little threads of selfish need that she clung to—all hope was destroyed.

Chapter Six

"You need to get your dumb ass off this ranch right now, or I will take this gun and shove it up your lily-white ass." Zeb thrust the tip of the shotgun up, mimicking his threat. He glared out at Dane from under the brim of his brand new cowboy hat. "You have no goddamned business being out here. You gave up that right."

Dane stood behind the cover of the driver's side door of the patrol car staring up at his brother as Zeb wrapped his arm around the shotgun and lifted a can of green snuff from his pocket. With an air of nonchalance, he took a dip and stuffed it into his lip, creating a bulge under his bottom lip.

The snow slid down off the roof of the house and fell with a wet thud to the ground just left of the porch where Zeb stood holding the gun. Same white house, same white picket fence, and the same bullshit Dane had always put up with as a child—while Zeb went on being his normal overly charming self.

Zeb lifted the gun from under his arm and pointed it in the direction of the car.

"Put the gun down, Zeb." His voice carried the edge of a practiced cop—the definite tone of don't-fuck-with-me mixed with I'll-shoot-you-if-you-even-try-to-move. As he pointed the gun straight at his brother's forehead, he forced himself not to smile. Sometimes this job felt so right it hurt.

"You wouldn't shoot me, little Danish…" Zeb chuckled as he stepped behind the porch's banister. "You don't have the balls to do a real man's job. You're nothing but a sniveling little boy—hell, that's all you've ever been."

His skin bristled with the jabs his brother threw at him, but he had a job to do—and it wasn't to be ruffled by his older, belligerent brother. "I'll ask you one more time. Put the gun down."

Zeb spat into the almost pristine white snow. "Enjoying your role as a big boy, are you?" The gun flagged lazily toward the passenger-side of the car. "I see you have my little trespasser in the car with you. I hadn't planned on pressing charges…but since you got her here…and after her little incident with Dancer…Well, I think I just changed my mind."

Aura squirmed in the passenger seat.

"Forget to tell me something?" Dane whispered under his breath as he flashed her an angry glance.

She looked over at him with a guilty twinkle in her eye. "I might have left a few things out, but he was the real criminal for letting his hand beat his horse. I didn't think you would be bringing me back here. You should've warned me."

Now wasn't the time to get in an argument with one of his… what was she? A witness or a suspect?

He stared up at Zeb. The bastard had a self-righteous smirk on his face as if he knew he had caused contention between Dane and Aura. The man loved a good fight.

"Listen, Zeb…If you don't put that gun down right now, I will be forced to put a non-lethal shotgun round into your chest. From what I hear, they aren't too pleasant."

The tip of Zeb's gun lowered, but came to a stop at the level of the bottom of the banister.

"Zeb, why don't you just listen instead of being an asshole?"

His sergeant would undoubtedly have something to say about the way he was handling the situation, but Dane didn't let it get to him. There was only one way to handle his brother. And if Sergeant Tester wanted to get up in arms about the situation, the next time he could come himself—he knew their history and Dane's well-placed hatred, yet he'd sent him anyway.

The gun thumped as Zeb sat it down against the top banister of the deck. Zeb stepped out onto the front step like an everyday perpetrator. "You gonna arrest me now? I was just playing with you, you know." He lifted his hands and laced his fingers behind his head.

Dane wanted to run up there and throw his brother to the ground, but his father's words rolled through his mind like an old scratchy record. *"He'll always be your brother, boy. Blood is thicker than water."*

Some ghosts he could never outrun, no matter how hard he tried.

"I don't think flagging me down with a gun is 'just playing.' You're lucky I didn't shoot your stupid ass." Dane stepped out from behind the open door and made his way toward the gun that rested on the porch. He walked past the man and picked up the discarded weapon. The barrel was clear.

"See? It wasn't even loaded." He jabbed toward the gun with his elbow. "Can I put my hands down now?"

Dane ignored his plea. Zeb deserved to be uncomfortable for a while—and Dane had every right to arrest the gray-haired paunch-bellied man in front of him.

"I need you to answer some questions for me." Dane pulled his notepad from his pocket. "I found some interesting things outside of the ranch that I think you might be able to help me with."

Zeb's bushy eyebrow shot up. "Like what? I heard about the hand at the lake. This wouldn't have anything to do with that, would it?"

His brother had always had a knack at getting under his skin and reading his mind—both abilities pissed him off in equal amounts. He tried to play it off. "I'll be asking the questions. You just need to answer. Do we understand each other?"

Zeb's port-belly jiggled as he laughed. "Whatever you say, little brother."

The words "little brother" dug at him and Zeb knew it—it had always pissed Dane off to be less-than—to always be trying to break out of his brother and father's abyssal shadows. "You haven't seen Angela lately, have you?"

Zeb's smug grin disappeared faster than a bunch of kids at a vandalism call. "Is she in some kind of trouble?"

"When's the last time you saw your wife?"

"She hasn't run back to you with some sob story, has she? I told her if she didn't get a handle on her drinking she was out." Zeb got a disgusted look on his face as he spat the words. "That's the God's honest truth. I put her out on her ass. She knew it was coming."

Dane twisted his brother's shotgun in his hands and inspected the cherry-colored worn wood—it had been their father's. His brother was an asshole, but would he have gone so far as to hurt Angela?

"When was that, Zeb?"

"Two weeks ago...Maybe two and a half. I don't know for sure."

He tried to gauge his brother's honesty based on his answers. He couldn't let his own hatred get in the way. "You can put your hands down."

Zeb unlaced his fingers and dropped his arms to his sides, shaking them out. The gun's butt dropped down to the porch with a dull thud and he leaned it against the post.

"What's going on, Dane?"

The door to the patrol car opened with a jarring screech. Aura stepped out, cell phone in hand. Dane's heart leapt up into his throat and his chest ached with pity and a strange tinge of protectiveness. He shouldn't have let her come here. To this place. To see this predacious man. Zeb could sense weakness like a wolf could smell a newborn calf.

"Aura, get back in the car."

"Oh look who it is. Hello, my little law-breaker. Did Dane tell you that you have an open invitation to dinner?"

Aura glared up at Zeb. "I wouldn't have dinner with you if you were the last man on earth."

Zeb laughed and his ample stomach bounced. "I should have known you would go and fuck my brother. You want to watch out though…I hear he's got a little pecker. But then, what do you care…You're nothing, just a little law-breaker. And nothing but trouble."

Aura charged past the door. "Look, you—"

"Aura. No. He's only trying to piss you off." Dane stepped between her and Zeb. "Please go back to the car. I will find out everything we need to know. This won't be the last time we have a chance to talk to him. Don't get upset."

"Run along, little lady." Zeb's smirk returned. "Listen to little Danish now. He's always looking after his *fillies*."

A look of shock flashed on Aura's face as if Zeb has slapped her instead of merely chided.

"That's *enough*." Dane pushed his brother back harder than he'd intended. "Leave her alone."

Zeb stared at her with a hungry wolf-like look in his eyes. "You and my brother aren't welcome on this place. You need to get the hell out of here."

Dane spun around to face his brother. "We'll leave in a second, but first I came up here to let you know that we found Angela's body. She was found along the deserted logging road to the north."

"No…" Zeb seemed to weaken and he stepped back. "You've got to be wrong. She's got to be fine. I just saw her…a couple of weeks ago." His face paled.

"I have a few questions for you. I'm going to need to take you back to the crime lab for you to identify the body."

Zeb ran his finger around his mouth, clearing away a piece of stringy brown chew that had escaped. "You know her as well as I do. You identify her."

Was Zeb being shifty because he was upset about Angela's death, or was he trying to avoid seeing her—avoiding some level of guilt?

"Is there a reason you don't want to come see her?"

"Look—I didn't have anything to do with her death." Zeb's eyes darkened and his cheeks seemed to take on a faint green hue. His lip pulled tight over the lump of chew in his mouth. "You know as well as I do that I loved that damned woman—for the good and the bad. I just wanted her to quit drinking. She said she was going to get cleaned up. Then she was coming back. I thought she meant she was going to some rehab clinic."

"She didn't make it to rehab."

"Son of a bitch." Zeb ran his hand along the brim of his cowboy hat. "What did she get herself into?"

"That's what I need to talk to you about. Do you know of any reason that someone would want her dead?" He pushed open the little pad of paper that he still held in his hand. The edges were rippled from the sweat of his palm.

He grabbed a pen from his pocket and clicked it open.

Zeb stared down at his pad of paper and pen with a look of annoyance, like Dane was out-of-line for telling him about her death, then hitting him up for suspects. But whether he liked it or not, it was part of Dane's job. Zeb was either going to comply now or Dane would be forced to bring him in for questioning.

He readied himself for the crap that would undoubtedly spill from his brother as he played his normal, manipulative power-play.

"I don't know. She'd been out a lot with her girlfriends. She'd been going to the bars."

"Any one in particular?"

"She'd been going down to a bar called Del's."

"How often was she going down there? About every night? Once a week?"

Aura stuffed her phone back in her purse and shoved her arms over her chest as she inspected Zeb. She looked every part as a cop. If only she could keep her emotions in check, she'd make one hell of a deputy.

Zeb looked up at the sky and let out a cloud as he exhaled. He brought his chin down. "I don't know. Probably about every night. You know the work at the ranch, Dane. I don't have time to babysit Angela."

His words rang false. When Dane had been married to Angela, a fair amount of his time had been spent following her around, trying to get her to come back home. The last time had been when he'd found her in the arms of Zeb. From that day on, the problem of Angela had fallen into his brother's lap.

"Well, you're done babysitting her." He turned to the car and then looked back over his shoulder at the wolf standing at the front of his den. "And don't worry about identifying her…I'll take care of it. I'd hate to make you go out of your way for your *wife*."

Chapter Seven

The black and white sheriff's car pulled up next to Aura in the Montana State Crime Lab parking lot. It had been a long ride from Somers to Missoula, but it had given her plenty of time to think—and to form a plan. She would glean whatever information she could from the crime lab then she'd go after Natalie—on her own if she had to. She'd wasted too much time already.

Dane tapped on her window. She looked up as he opened the door.

For a moment she was back lying on the ground, him on top of her in the Diamond's pasture, and the frosty tendrils of grass rubbing against her lust-warmed face. He was looking at her with a sparkle of want in his eyes. His body was hard against her as she slowly raised her hips, seducing, needing, wanting him to be against her. Like the men she'd seduced in her past, she had seen the sexually starved way his body disobeyed his mind as he'd driven hard against her. There was emotion within him, somewhere deep, somewhere hidden, somewhere that she may never have the chance to experience again.

Stop. I can't think of him like this. I have to focus on Natalie. She needs me. I can't have…love.

"You know you didn't have to come down here, Aura. I called in a favor to get in before the results are finalized—they may not have anything of use to find Natalie."

His words pulled her from her fantasy. "Hello to you too, Dane. It's nice to see you. Yes, my trip was fine." Her words took on the finely sharpened edge of a well-honed knife.

He looked at her and frowned. "Yeah, sorry…*Hi.*"

"Hi." She smiled, lips tight. "There was no way you were going to keep me from coming down here. If there is something on that phone I need to know about it. I need to know who she called besides me."

"I get it, Aura. I get what you are trying to do—saving your sister and all. But this isn't just about her. This isn't just about those women. There is something more going on and we need to get to the bottom of it."

Aura grabbed her purse from the seat beside her. "That's exactly what I'm trying to do." *And while I'm at it, I'm going to find my sister.*

"I don't know what happens down in Arizona, or what your judgments are about law enforcement in Montana—but even here we don't believe in vigilante justice. You can't go out on your own to find your sister. You are welcome to work with me, but I can't have you contaminating any more crime scenes or messing up my investigation."

"I won't mess up your investigation." That was the last thing she'd want—to put Natalie's life even further into danger.

"It's not just about the investigation—you can't go running around hunting down the people who did this. If you get hurt—"

"You'd have more paperwork to do…I know." Aura stepped out of her pickup and slammed the door.

"Stop, Aura. You know that's not what I meant." Dane's hand moved instinctively to his waist, where his utility belt normally rested. Instead he was wearing what she assumed to be his every day wear—crisply ironed blue jeans and a collared maroon, silver, and white University of Montana polo shirt.

If she hadn't been so damned irritated with him, he would have looked…She glanced back at him. No, he *was* strikingly handsome.

"I don't care what you meant," she lied. Her heels pounded on the ground as she made her way to the front door of the unassuming brown county building. "Let's go."

The putrid odor of death twisted around the refrigerated crime lab, assaulting her nostrils and clinging to her like an unwelcome spirit. She wanted to run. To get out of this place and away from the defiling stink that permeated her clothing and hair.

Aura clutched her purse tight. This was for Natalie and to find out exactly what was on that purple phone that flaunted its god-awful cheeriness. She needed to find out for herself exactly what she was going to be dealing with.

Dane touched the door that read *Authorized Personnel Only,* which led to the main lab, then stopped. He turned back and looked at her. "You can't come in here. You'll have to wait in the lobby."

It had been a long night envisioning Angela's little black horse tattoo—and the way it matched her own. Every time she'd thought she was close to sleep, she'd close her eyes only to fall into whirling dreams of whipping snow and zigzagging snowshoe hares—all leading to the dead face of Natalie.

She wouldn't leave without the answers she needed—that her sister was still alive—and that those cruel visions had only been figments of an overactive and stressed imagination.

"I'm coming into the lab with you."

"Dr. Redbird won't allow it. She's—"

"I'm *coming with you.* Tell her I'm a trainee or something. I don't care." She stepped next to him.

He opened his mouth to retort, but for a second she let him stare at her. Nothing he could say would stop her.

She pushed the cold metal door. It swung open lightly as if it was used to having regular newcomers to the halls of the morgue.

"Fine. Stay quiet." Dane stepped in front of her and led the way down the sterile glaring-white hallway.

On their left was a stairwell. Next to it on the wall was a framed placard which listed the departments within the crime lab and the floors where they could be found. She read down from the top:

Floor three: Photography Section, Evidence Storage Section, Identification Section.

Floor two: Firearms Section, Instrument Section.

Floor one: Chemistry Section, General Examination Section, Main Offices.

The elevator dinged on the other side of the hall and she sped up, catching up to Dane who was three steps ahead.

They walked past a door that read *Toxicology Lab*. Inside was machine after machine, each standing as stoic reminders of the hundreds of cases that the lab had on their hands. The pit in the bottom of her stomach grew. There were so many stories out there that ended here at this office-like center of death and possible answers.

Their footsteps echoed off the tiles as they made their way to the end of the hall and the door that read *Autopsy Suite*—like it was some kind of hotel for the dead. Chills ran down her spine.

Dane peered into the small bulletproof window of the door. He gave a curt nod to someone inside, then looked back at Aura. "Are you sure you wanna do this?"

She swallowed back the sour flavor in her mouth.

He opened the door and she followed him inside. At the far end of the room a small inconspicuous brunette woman hunched over, poking at a pale hand that sat lifeless on the cold-looking steel. Dane cleared his throat. She looked up from her work. Her face was covered by a plastic shield and mask, perfectly matching her blue paper gown and slippers that protected her from the foul contents that came with rotting flesh.

"Dr. Redbird, we're sorry to interrupt your work. I just wanted to come by and see what you've found from the bodies. I know it's only been a day since you got them, but is there any information you've gathered? Any evidence of what exactly we've got on our hands?"

"Hello, Deputy Burke." The mousy woman sat down the little set of scissors and stepped back from the hand. "Long time no see. I'm glad you made the trip—I found some really interesting peculiarities that might be useful in your investigation." She smiled warmly to Dane, then her gaze flashed to Aura and her smile disappeared. "Who's your friend, Dane?"

Aura mentally cringed at the overly friendly way the woman said his name—like she was marking him as hers, and not to be touched.

"This is a friend of mine, Aura Montgarten. She's from a department out of Arizona. Hope you don't mind. She's aiding in the investigation." The lie flew from his lips with the practiced grace of a Las Vegas magician.

"Pleasure." The doctor pulled at the edges of her gloves and pulled them off, inside out. "Well, we haven't finished up with the toxicology reports or the DNA analysis, but as luck has it for you, we haven't been too busy this week and I could get right to the post-mortem examination."

Yes, it was a lucky day when there were fewer dead bodies.

"Find anything interesting?" Dane's voice took on a softer edge.

The medical examiner removed her plastic face shield, revealing a young twenty-something woman—far from the mousy woman Aura had first judged the woman to be. "It's my belief that we're most likely dealing with a homicide, as your notes seemed to assume from the crime scene. However, there were a few peculiarities." The woman nodded, making her full ponytail bounce to life.

A tingle of jealousy swept through Aura as she noticed the way the doctor seemed to focus on the small, almost imperceptible, cleft at the center of Dane's chiseled jaw.

"On both victims we found traces of the tarp as well as some interesting non-human type hair."

"Do you know what type of hair it was? Canine?"

A lump formed in Aura's throat as she remembered the little square of tissue that rested in the pocket of yesterday's jeans. The hair wouldn't be canine—or truly equine either.

The woman walked to the far side of the room to a stainless steel lab table where a bag lay. Inside were a few strands of long, black hairs. She lifted up the bag to the light.

"It appears to be the coarse hair from a horse's tail, but under the microscope the cuticle, or the scaly exterior of the hair, seems to be rougher than that of something of an equine source. It seems almost human-ish." She squinted at the hair as if it would magically somehow make sense if she just stared a little while longer. "If I hadn't gotten the whole strand along with the follicle, I would have thought it possible that it was a woman's hair."

Aura smiled but kept her mouth shut.

Dane pulled out his little notepad that he seemed to always have on hand. He jotted down a few notes as the woman twisted the bag in her fingers.

Aura peeked over and noticed he had written *Possibly brought in by horse?*

The doctor twisted the bag in her fingers as if she was trying to make sense of the anomaly. "Also, Angela had wounds on her back which were at the initial stages of healing at the time of her death that look similar to the burn marks on her disarticulated hand."

"What kind of wounds?"

The doctor glanced over at Dane. "They look like possible rope burns, but it's hard to say."

"What about the tarp?" Dane asked, not looking up from his paper.

"Well, from what I can tell the tarp is just the standard everyday blue tarp you can buy at any big box store. I don't know how helpful it's going to be in nailing down a perpetrator." She sat the bag back down. "Did you have a chance to examine the bodies before they came in?"

Dane coughed lightly as if the question made him uncomfortable.

Aura wasn't sure if it was the question, or the fact that one of the women they'd found had been his ex-wife, that made him more uncomfortable. It amazed her that he could be so distant when it came to investigating the deaths. If she had been married to one of the victims she would have had a hard time dealing with their dead body, but Dane seemed to take it in stride.

Dane looked up from his tablet and scratched the thin layer of stubble that grew over his tanned chin. "I only got a chance to get a look at the second victim, the one under the tarp. We still haven't managed to come up with any identification. Have you had anyone come in who can ID her?"

The woman shook her head. "Not yet. We haven't released Angela's name to the public either. We still need to notify her mother and father. Have you had the chance to talk to them?"

"She doesn't have any that I know of. She said they passed away when she was in high school." He stopped scratching. "Did you manage to find the cause of death?"

Dr. Redbird picked up her clipboard and flipped through some pages. "As you know, Angela was missing her hand." She looked over the clipboard and eyed Dane. He nodded and her gaze slipped back down to the paper. "From the tests we've run I can say with one hundred percent certainty that the hand did belong to Angela Burke. I assume this is *your* Angela, correct?"

"My brother's Angela…but yes. I knew her."

"I'll take that as a positive identification." The doctor wrote something down. "About the hand…From what I've seen on both the body and the hand itself, it seems as if the wound was caused perimortem, or at or around the time of death. There were no signs of healing and the body showed staining on the radioulnar joint where the hand had been removed."

Dane's pen moved furiously over the paper. "Can you tell what exactly removed the hand? It looked a little indistinct in the water."

"The margins were, as you said, indistinct. It clearly wasn't removed from the body with a sharp object." The doctor scanned further down her clipboard. "The peripheral tissue on the hand and the arm showed no level of edema—which could mean that the tissue didn't have time to swell after the appendage was removed." Dr. Redbird reached over and patted his arm.

Dane seemed to go rigid under the woman's touch.

"If it makes you feel better, the hand could have been removed after the time of death. She might not even have felt it." The doctor dropped her hand.

"That's nice." Dane seemed to squirm away from her as he went back to his notepad.

"Oh...yes, I also located some interesting traces on the wrist tissue of the body. There were what appeared to be yellow and green nylon fibers. I'm hypothesizing that it's possible they belonged to some type of rope—though they could come from a carpet or rug—it's hard to tell without more time."

Her assertion was met with the scratch of Dane's pen. "So what exactly was the cause of death? Officer Grant didn't seem to think there was any evidence of blunt or sharp force trauma. Did you find any evidence of a gunshot wound that he may have missed?"

"No...No gunshots, but both women had clear defense wounds on their forearms and hands. But aside from those wounds, and a few bruises to the necks and torsos, I didn't find any direct evidence that would indicate the cause of death." She flipped the page on the clipboard to a little diagram of a body surrounded by notes. "Neither presented to me any evidence of a natural death. It's strange. But once we get the toxicology reports they could tell us what the cause of death might be."

She pulled out a manila envelope from the back of the clipboard and handed it to Dane. "Here's what we have so far, so you can take a look."

"What about the phone?" Aura said.

Dr. Redbird stared at her with disdain, as if Aura had interrupted a private interlude that was happening between her and Dane— one that Aura had no right witnessing.

Dane flipped the manila bag in his hands and shook his head as he subtly reminded Aura to remain silent. Something flashed in his eyes. The light wasn't anger or frustration...no. It was something different, something primordial and animalistic—as if he was her master.

"The purple phone. Pink flowers. Did you find any data that would be helpful in the investigation?" Aura asked as she smiled mischievously over at Dane. He should have known by now that he couldn't make her submit to his will.

Dr. Redbird nodded. "The phone's in the bag. You'll need to sign it out before you take it back to your station." The doctor motioned to Dane's envelope. "We weren't able to pull any prints, but we finally got it working. There was a video that you might find of some interest."

"Great." Dane took a step between the doctor and Aura, stopping her from interloping again without his permission.

"Yes," Aura said, stepping to his side. "We'll make sure to take a look."

She was a nymph. A Mustang. Wild and free. No man or god would ever be her master.

Chapter Eight

Painfully slowly, the purple cell phone flickered to life. The background was a picture of horses running through a meadow, their manes flowing in the wind.

"Is it on?" Aura leaned over the computer that sat bolted over the center console within the patrol car. "Oh. Great. Here, let me take a look."

"Aura." He pulled the phone back so she couldn't see it. "Do I really need to remind you who is the investigating officer?"

She sat back and pushed her arms over her chest. "Okay, *investigating officer*. Investigate." She motioned to the phone with a sardonic grin.

Little circles lined up over the screen and above them read *Draw pattern to unlock*. His cheeks burned. If he was back at the station, one of the IT guys could have shown him how to bypass the pain-in-the-ass lock. Except he wasn't at the station; instead, here he was locked in the patrol car with a woman who seemed to want to show him what an idiot he could be.

Aura's smile widened as a knowing sparkle lit up her blue eyes. Why did she have to look at him like that? All he was trying to do was find out who was behind the murders, where Natalie was, and if they had more victims—yet, all Aura seemed to care about was the need to chide him with her sexy little sneer.

He tried a few swipes to unlock the phone then begrudgingly handed it over. "Here."

She reached over to him and as her fingers wrapped around the phone, she accidently twisted her finger around his. Her hand was warm, too warm—as if she was nervous about being in an enclosed car with him.

Her cheeks flushed a faint pink and she pulled the phone out of his fingers. "Thanks." She tapped the screen and the main screen opened. "You have to do it like this." She tapped the precise code in and handed him the phone.

"Thanks." He took the phone and opened the phone log. "It's says here that the last call was to you. It looks like it was only fifteen seconds long. Does that sound right?"

"I just heard a woman talking and then the phone line went dead. I tried to call her back, but it went straight to voicemail. So I tracked the phone's GPS, which led me to Shirley Mountain, but that's as close as I could get her location." Aura nodded. "Let's find that video—maybe we can find more. Or what she was doing up on the mountain."

"Yeah, the video." He couldn't tear his gaze away from her smoldering pink lips, so pink that they silently begged to be kissed. What would it have been like to finish what they had started back on the grass of the Diamond?

He tapped the screen until he found the newest video.

"You son of a bitch, Shawn!" a dark-haired woman yelled.

"Why the hell did you run from me?" a man's voice answered.

It was hard to see anything as the grainy video bounced around and must have been shuffled around in the owner's grip.

"You lied to me...to us. And now you want us to do *what?*" The woman's voice carried an edge of terror.

Was *Shawn* the man they were looking for?

The video moved jerkily and for a second, in the background, was a large chestnut-colored bay standing beside a scratched up tree. The horse's nostrils were flared and its eyes wide. The video jerked down and there was a woman's shrill scream.

The video stopped.

He couldn't dismiss the feeling that they had just been witness to the beginnings of a homicide. Hopefully they hadn't just witnessed Natalie's murder.

From the little amount of scenery that he'd seen in the video, it looked like the clip had been taken somewhere here in Montana. He stared down at the phone. The date matched when Aura said she'd last talked to her sister. The chills spilled down his spine.

"Was that Natalie's voice?"

"No…I don't think so." Something about Aura's wide eyes reminded him of the bay in the video—she had the same big eyes, the same flowing hair—and the same look of terror.

He swallowed down the bitter taste that filled his mouth. "Do you know any guys named Shawn?"

"That's…that's her ex-husband." Her face blanched.

"What else haven't you told me?"

She stared at him for a long minute like she wanted to tell him something, as if something burned inside of her, begging to be released.

"All I know was that she was seeing a new guy. I think his name was Ryan. She hadn't said anything about Shawn—but I guess it's possible that he didn't like the idea of her dating someone new."

Finally, a suspect. "Do you know where Shawn lives?"

"I don't know where Shawn's living now…the last time I saw him was about six months ago in Flagstaff." Aura reached over and put her hand on his leg. "I know Shawn—I don't think he would ever do anything like this. He might get angry, but he'd never kill anyone."

His heart jumpstarted in his chest as her fingers brushed the inside of his thigh. "Aura, you'd be surprised what a man could do when he's angry."

She squeezed his leg. "There are very few things that can surprise me."

"What's Shawn's last name?"

"Gunner."

He typed the name in to the computer as he tried to ignore the fact that her hand was still resting on his thigh. The man's information popped up on the computer screen, but that was it—no criminal record, no major red flags. From a scan of the man's background he seemed like any other civilian—he held a standard nine to five job in Flagstaff, owned a house and a silver GMC truck. Nothing that he'd expect to find on a murderer, but then again he'd learned to never trust what that little black screen said. There were plenty of people that had skeletons piled up under their mattresses.

"What about this Ryan? Do you know his last name?"

Aura nibbled at her lip. "I think it's Patrick."

Dane scanned down, Ryan popped up. He clicked on the contact. "Patrick. Ryan Patrick. Here it says he lives in Somers." His gut clenched with excitement at their first truly strong lead. They could have someone that would know more about Natalie's disappearance.

He punched the name into his computer that rested between the two front seats of the patrol car. Ryan's name and last known address popped up onto the screen. Dane's stomach dropped as he read the familiar address—of the Diamond.

"Is Ryan a ranch hand for Zeb?"

Aura's hand clenched tight on his thigh. "I don't know—I guess it's possible. She never really talked about what he did besides bronc riding. They'd only met a few times and then talked online."

"Your sister dates men she meets online?" His internal alarm squealed.

"It's nothing like that. She met him at a rodeo a few years back, when she was married and he was only a friend. They'd kept in touch. He's moved around a bit until he found his way up here to Montana. I knew he worked as a cattle hand, but I didn't know he worked for your brother."

He dropped his hand to Aura's and wrapped his fingers around hers. The warmth of her skin seeped into him, warming the layer of ice that had formed around his heart at the time of his divorce and had only thickened since. "We'll find Natalie. We'll get whoever is going after these women."

"Promise me." Aura leaned close to him and the scent of her floral perfume wafted from the soft-looking skin of her neck.

"What?" He stared at the little hole at the base of her throat.

"Promise me that you will do everything in your power to find my sister." She moved closer and her lips stopped next to his.

"I'll never let anything happen to you." He took in a long breath, breathing in her essence. "I'll do anything to protect you."

He couldn't stop himself. He had to possess those lips that were so close to his. He took her lips with his, tasting the sweetness of her lipstick as he ran his tongue against her full bottom lip. Blood raced through him making his body quiver to life. She took control of the kiss, pulling and sucking on his flesh. Desire flooded him. He needed to feel her against him.

"Dane..." she said, her moist breath caressing his lips. "I... we...need to go. Natalie."

He closed his eyes. She was right. They couldn't be doing this. He needed to keep his objectivity. There was a case to be solved.

He followed Aura back to Somers, keeping a comfortable distance between the patrol car and her truck. If only he could keep this kind of distance between them all the time, there would be none of the questions that seemed to be on a constant roll through his mind. There was no way he could have a relationship with her. There were too many speed bumps—she was no longer a suspect, but she was still a vital part of the investigation. If something happened—something more than what had already transpired—the investigation would be compromised. That wasn't a risk that he could take. There were possible lives at stake.

Two and a half hours later and arriving back at Somers, he rolled up next to her at the only stop light in town. He motioned for her to roll down her window.

"Let's go to the Diamond."

She nodded and slid her window shut. Dane followed her down the snow-covered road that led to the ranch.

The patrol car bounced down the long winding driveway until he pulled up to the white house where Zeb's truck was parked. The porch stood unoccupied—at least this time they weren't met with his brother toting a firearm. Hopefully he would be as welcoming when it came to them asking for access to the Forest Service land.

He threw the car into park and stepped up on the porch stair to wait for Aura. The dogs barked from the backyard and in the pasture to the left of the house, a few cows lazily nosed through the snow to get to whatever grass remained. It seemed quiet for the ranch—a little *too* quiet.

"Where's Zeb?" Aura asked.

Dane shrugged and turning, sprinted up the steps to the front door and banged on the lion-shaped knocker. Silence. No footsteps, no television, nothing. He pressed his face to the glass and peered inside. The lights were off. He tried to ignore the concern that crept into his psyche. Zeb was fine. He was probably out in his office, or out talking to Pat about what needed to be done next. There were more than enough reasons that he wouldn't be home in the middle of the day.

"Let's head to the barn, maybe he's over there," Aura said.

She climbed in the patrol car and they drove the half mile to the barn. A red and white truck was parked outside the double doors.

"Whose truck is that?" Aura asked.

Dane shrugged. He'd seen it around town, but he'd never paid it much notice. With as many tourists and seasonal residents that lived in Somers it was hard to keep track of all the comings and goings.

His instincts took control and he put his hand to his sidearm as he pushed open the red door of the barn. Aura stepped behind him and the cover of the second door. "Is anyone in here?" he yelled.

The sound of metal banging against metal echoed out into the barnyard. Someone was inside. "Zeb?" he yelled again, as he moved to look inside the door.

A man stood behind a huge metal vise, a sledgehammer in his hand, and green hearing protectors over his ears. "Hey!" Dane yelled, trying to get the man's attention.

The man looked up. "Hello?" He sat the sledgehammer down and pulled the protectors off. "What's up?" He gave them a puzzled look.

"Hey, I'm Deputy Burke." Dane dropped his hand from his sidearm. "We're looking for Zeb, you seen him?"

"Hey, I'm Pat's son, Ryan."

The weighted silence hung in the air. "You're Ryan…Ryan *Patrick*?" Dane said.

"The one and only." Ryan walked over to him and stuck out his gloved hand. Dane gave it a strong shake. The young man seemed centered, put together, and completely oblivious as to why a Deputy Sheriff would be standing with him in a barn.

Aura pushed through the door behind him. "Ryan?" she said with an edge of desperation in her voice. "I'm Aura…Natalie's sister. I tried to call you."

"Aura…" Ryan smiled too warmly, making Dane's hackles rise. "Natalie's talked so much about you." He reached over and wrapped his arms around her.

"Hey now," Dane said, grabbing the man's shoulder in warning. The man could be a killer—he had no business touching her. "Step back."

Aura's cheek turned the color of an over-ripened apple and he dropped his hand from the man.

"*Dane.*" She wiggled free of the man's arms.

The young kid glanced over, his smile never wavering. "It's alright. If someone I didn't know was touching Natalie, I'd do the same thing."

"Ryan, have you seen her?"

"Well…" He stared down at his feet. "She and I had a fight a few days ago. I haven't heard from her since. I thought she'd gone back down south."

"What did you two fight about?" Dane lost the edge of civility in his voice, only to be replaced with the authority of his many days on the force.

The young man's smile disappeared. "Are you really going to pull bad cop on me, Deputy? My old man told me all about you and your brother."

"Stop. Right. There." Dane growled. "We're not here to talk about me. We're here to find out where your ex is—and if you had anything to do with her disappearance."

"If you're implying that I had something to do with her going missing you're dead wrong. I love Natalie…" The man stabbed his boot into the hay-covered dirt of the barn floor.

"That's what most suspects say when a girl goes missing."

"Do they all ask the girl to marry them too?" Ryan threw his gloves on the floor. "This is bullshit. I had nothing to do with her disappearance. Goddamn it, I didn't even know she was missing!" One of the horses from the back stalls whinnied nervously as the man raised his voice.

"He's telling the truth," Aura said, as she stared off in the direction of the horse. "He *loved* her."

The way she said the word "loved" made it sound like it belonged down in the muck of the barn floor. What did she have against love? Or was it something else she had a problem with—him?

He stopped. He was being overly sensitive and far too emotional. Letting his emotions boil to the surface was out-of-line, especially when he was dealing with a potential suspect.

"Do you know of anyone else who would have had cause to harm Natalie? Anyone who was upset with her?" He tried to regain his objectivity.

Ryan knelt down and picked up his gloves. "Look, all I know was that I told her that I loved her. That I wanted to marry her. Then she up and ran off. I tried to go after her, but she'd already taken all of her stuff out of my house and hit the road. Or so I thought."

"Where's your house, Ryan?"

"I'm staying up with my old man. Up on Twin Lakes Road." He pointed north.

Twin Lakes Road was only two miles from where they'd found the women's bodies. Had the kid killed the women after he'd been rejected by Natalie? Had he murdered in a fit of rage?

"What did you do after Natalie left?"

Aura looked over at him and frowned, as if chastising him for asking more questions. He had to ignore her—and the way her eyes seemed to grow brighter when she was angry, almost as if he'd lit a fire behind them.

Ryan turned on his heel and moved to a bin of grain that sat next to the long work bench that was built into the front of the barn. "I was pissed. I admit it. At first I wanted to chase after her. Run her down. Find her. Make her come back." He sat his gloves down and perched on the edge of the bin. He looked haggard—like a man after a break-up and too many nights alone. "Aura, you know Natalie. Once she makes her mind up, there's no changing it. So after she left, I stayed here. Worked on fences for a while, then headed down to Del's for a beer."

The kid seemed to hunch so low that it looked like he was shrinking. It was easy to see that he told the truth. The kid was heartbroken—that was a feeling Dane knew and could recognize all too well.

"Why did she say she wouldn't marry you?" He should have left the kid alone, and let Ryan's wounds heal, but that wasn't his job. He needed to know the whole truth in order to find answers.

"She said we were too different." Ryan picked at the edge of the plywood box. "Whatever the hell that means."

"Don't beat yourself up, Ryan." Aura stepped over beside him and sat her hand on his shoulder. "Natalie has a tendency to do things like this. It has nothing to do with you. I know she thought a lot of you…that's probably why she—" She stopped.

"Why she *what*?" Dane asked.

"Nothing. She's just flighty, that's all." Aura's cheeks tinged with pink. "It's the Bohemian in her. She never stays in one place or with one man for long."

Dane tried to hold back, but his emotions formed words and poured out of his mouth before he could stop them. "Are you like your sister?"

Her pink cheeks turned crimson. "Now isn't the time, Dane."

She was right. Why hadn't he kept his damn mouth shut?

He turned back to Ryan. "We have a video, if you don't mind taking a look." He pulled Natalie's phone from his pocket and opened the clip.

The man stared at the phone as the scene unfolded.

"I know this place…It's not far from here. Look here." Ryan paused the video and pointed to a tree behind the startled horse. "See that pine? That's a bear rubbing tree."

Dane scanned the photo. Long scratches scarred the bark of the tree that stood next to the horse. "Can you take us there?"

Chapter Nine

The saddle creaked as Aura bent down to miss a branch that flexed low under the snow. The mountain trail was barely six inches wide with thick bushes and trees to her left and a steep bush-covered decline to her right. She couldn't quit thinking about Zeb and how he had called her a *filly* the last time they had spoken. Did he know the truth about her and his ex-wife?

She had to believe Zeb didn't know, or he would have never let Ryan talk him into letting them borrow the horses and travelling onto the mountain. At the very least, Zeb mustn't have known anything of the truth of the reason for their ride. Regardless, she was thankful to get the chance to finally investigate Natalie's last known location.

The black gelding she rode laid its ears back. It huffed as she sat back up. Since she'd worked with Dancer, it was easy to tell Pat had been at his old ways and Aura could feel the resentment and hatred seeping up from the horse's flesh. Dancer yearned to be free—to run without reins, without a bit, and without a master. She stopped the horse and stepped down from the saddle, careful not to slip on the wash of ice-covered stones that littered the trail.

The gelding snorted impatiently, hating to be left behind from its herd. The horse Dane rode on neighed back, answering with its own impatience.

"Shh…" she whispered, running her hands down the horse's neck. Its nostrils flared as it took in the scents around them. "It's okay, Dancer," she crooned.

Aura ran her fingers up to the horse's white forelock and rubbed slowly, letting her energy seep through her fingers and into the horse's mind. It only took a few seconds before his eyes glazed over.

Have you seen my sister, she's a horse-shifter—a pretty bay? Aura thought. *Her name's Natalie.*

The horse stared at her. *Yes... We ran together. She was scared.*

Of what?

A man...

Aura tried to control her excitement. They were close—they would find Natalie. They had to. She rubbed her fingers under the front of the horse's mane. *Who?*

Her mate.

What did he look like? Aura tried again.

Dancer drew back from her fingers, breaking the connection. She reached up again, but the horse stepped back and looked around her.

"Aura?" The sound of Dane's voice broke her concentration. She turned to see him sitting high in the saddle on the trail in front of her. He smiled brilliantly, the picture of a stunning cowboy as he sat on the beautiful roan mare. "What're you doing?"

She dropped her hand and smiled. "Nothing. Just needed to stretch my legs."

"You, the woman who seems more comfortable with horses than humans, needs to get off the horse to stretch her legs? Ryan told me about what you did with Pat and that horse." He looked at her with disbelief.

He and Ryan must have been talking. At least it was an improvement from the way Dane had seemed to instantly dislike the young man. She couldn't decide whether it was because he was a possible, but unlikely, suspect or if Dane disliked him for the air of sexuality that seemed to come off Ryan.

"Hey, you guys coming?" Ryan pushed past a tree and stopped his horse next to Dane. "We're running out of daylight."

Aura slipped her foot into the stirrup and pulled herself back up and into the saddle. "Let's go."

Ryan turned. "It's not much further."

If they had any luck at all they could find evidence of exactly what had happened to Natalie, but thanks to Dancer the circle of suspects had grown a little smaller. There were only two men that were involved in her sister's life—the man that led their group and Shawn—the man's voice in the video. Shawn had to be the one responsible for Natalie's disappearance. Maybe he had been upset that she'd gone with Ryan. Maybe he was upset about her leaving him. Or maybe they'd had a fight, Natalie had accidently filmed it, and she and Shawn had made up—maybe they had simply run away.

The chills ran up her spine like a trail of spiders. Natalie wasn't okay. She was being stupid to think that Natalie was anything less than in mortal danger. The only thing she could hope for was that her sister was still alive—that she wasn't like those girls lying in the morgue, being poked and prodded by the little gloved hands of the brunette that seemed to have had a thing for Dane. She shivered in her thick down jacket.

Dancer snorted nervously. His body tensed beneath Aura's legs. Something was wrong.

The brush rustled ahead of Ryan. His horse's nostrils flared as it snorted and its ears pointed at the rustling bush. A black form slunk through the brush, barely visible.

The horse jerked under Ryan's legs and he tried to calm her, but it was no use as the horse danced around, trying to get out of the danger zone.

A black wolf jumped out from the scrub, its teeth gnashed together as a deep snarling growl rippled from its throat. Its ribs were visible beneath its ragged, mangy-looking coat as it moved in front of Ryan's horse and lunged toward the horse's throat. The mare's front legs rose from the ground as it reared back. Ryan tried to hold on as the horse lurched beneath him. The mare reared again, catching him off guard, and its head connected with the bridge of Ryan's nose with a blood-chilling crunch. The man slumped.

The horse stomped at the wolf, its violent action throwing the unconscious Ryan around in the saddle like a ragdoll.

The wolf moved to Aura's left and moved behind Dane's horse and lunged toward the horse's hamstrings. The horse kicked, just missing the wolf's snarling mouth. Dane twisted in the saddle as he looked back to her. The horse kicked again at the wolf, upsetting his balance. A look of terror filled his eyes.

"Dane!" she cried.

His body moved to the left, away from the wolf, toward the mountain as the horse leapt to the right. The wolf lunged again only upsetting Dane further. His left foot slipped in the stirrup as his body slipped from the saddle. His body fell back as his hands grasped the air for something to grab to stop his fall. He grimaced as he flew downward. His head bounced off the flagstones that lay next to his horse's hooves and his face went blank. The mare jolted, pulling him underneath her belly. His foot was caught in the left stirrup. If the mare moved—if one solid footfall struck him—he would be gone.

"Whoa," Aura said, trying to send calming energies to the animals that shifted and circled around her. She jumped down out of the saddle. The wolf stopped and stared at her. She could feel it watching the pulse of her carotid artery, waiting for the perfect moment to strike the woman that had put herself in the prey zone.

She stared the beast down. Why hadn't she brought a gun? She looked over at Dane, searching for his gun. The firearm was out of sight, pinned too far out of reach.

"Shhh…" She slid her body toward Dane. Maybe she could reach the gun if she tried.

The black wolf eased its front paw off the ground and stepped forward, lowering its shoulders, stalking her. Her heart thundered in her chest, but she forced her body to stay under control. She couldn't run. She had to stay and fight—and protect Dane.

"Hey, baby…" She said as she put her hand on the horse's rump to let it know she was there. Reaching down, she pulled Dane's foot from the stirrup. The wolf stepped closer, its yellow eyes gleamed with anger. Behind the look of fury there was also a hunger, like she and Dane were simply tasty morsels of flesh wrapped in inconvenient clothing.

"No," she said, letting the word come up from the depths of her being, channeling her innermost alpha. "You will not touch him." She leaned down and lifted him by his arms and, with the strength that comes to mothers whose children are in peril, she moved him up the hillside and out from beneath the horse.

Dane's horse spooked and took off running up the trail. Ryan's mare followed closely at its heels, with the limp Ryan still in the saddle. "Whoa!" she yelled, trying to get the horses to stop, but it was no use—instinct had taken over.

The black wolf took the opening and ran at her, throwing its full weight against her chest. Her hands slipped out from beneath Dane's arms and she reached up to tear at the wild beast's throat. It latched onto her arm, ripping at her like she was a chew toy rather than a demi-god. She reached up with her free hand and grabbed its ear.

Stop! Now! Stop or I will kill you!

The beast stopped thrashing, but kept her flesh in its clenched teeth.

What? the beast thought, befuddled by the sudden invasion of its mind. *Shut up.*

It writhed again, trying to rip her flesh from bone. The pain coursed through her like a million needles as her nerves fired with pain. She pushed it back, letting the adrenaline that flowed through her system take over. Fight. Kill. Live.

I will kill you!

She showed no fear as she held onto its ear, refusing to break the bond.

Look, beast woman, you and your friends are going to die. Let go! The wolf pulled back, but she gripped tighter. The beast yelped with pain.

She jabbed her thumb into the wolf's eye and he jerked his head, but refused to let go of her arm. The pain radiated up from her arm, but she ignored it.

Dane groaned from the trail behind her as she played tug of war with her body. Down at his waist was his sidearm. She reached down and, unclipping the gun, pulled it from the holster. She pushed the tip of the barrel against the beast's forehead, right between his eyes.

Why did you attack us? Her finger trembled on the trigger. She pressed the tip harder against the animal's unyielding skull.

You're prey. You're nothing. A growl rippled from the wolf.

The words "you're nothing" echoed in her mind. Zeb had said those same words.

She pulled the trigger and the shocked beast released its jaws.

The gun clicked. Empty.

She let go of the wolf's ear and pulled back the slide as she loaded a bullet into the gun's chamber. The wolf leapt back. The wolf's back feet lost traction on the steep ice-covered decline. Fear filled its eyes as it scrambled to regain its footing. The rocks tumbled down the hill as the wolf kicked wildly. The animal's back feet slipped out from underneath its body. It slipped down the hill, only its head above the edge.

Aura lunged forward, grabbing the wolf by the nape of its neck. "You won't get away from me this easily." The wolf yelped as she pulled it to the safety of the narrow trail.

She let go of the beast's hackle and it turned on her, its lips turned up in what looked like a boxer's bloodied and victorious smile.

She lifted the gun as she staggered backward up the icy hillside. Dancer screamed as the wolf stepped toward her. The wolf turned just as the horse dropped its head and charged the enemy. With a well-placed stomp, Dancer smashed the beast to the ground. The wolf yelped, its sound a mixture of surprise, pain, and unbridled anger.

Dancer brought his feet down with a sickening thump. The sound stopped as the wolf's bloody body slipped over the edge of the trail and disappeared.

Chapter Ten

Tiny alarms sounded in his head. *Warning... Warning...* The cold jagged rocks poked into his back and his head throbbed. What had happened?

Dane forced himself up onto his elbows and looked down the narrow mountain trail. Aura and Ryan were gone. Were they okay? Had something happened to them as well?

He jumped to his feet. The alarms in his head turned into the throb of long wailing distress calls, like the tornado warnings he'd once heard in the Midwest. The world spun around him, twisting his stomach and forcing a roiling sickness to wash over him. He sat back down and dropped his head between his knees. He would be fine in a minute. He could get up and go looking for them.

What if something had happened to Aura?

Scarlet-red blood was splattered over the well-trodden white snow of the trail. On the downhill side there was a long smear of the sticky liquid which disappeared off the cliff. Where was Aura?

The nausea sucker-punched him in the gut, forcing him to drop his head back down between his knees. Aura was strong. Ryan would take care of her—unless Ryan was the man they were really looking for. Was it possible that Ryan could be the man responsible for the murder of Angela and the other unidentified woman? Ryan seemed innocent, and normally Dane's intuition was right, but what if he was wrong? A new sense of urgency took hold. He pushed to his feet, swaying slightly.

Dane reached down to his waist, instinctively checking his gun. The holster was empty.

"Aura?" His voice sounded reedy, like a young man desperate to find his lover.

He stumbled up the trail. The horses had stomped in the blood-colored snow, sending red slush splattering around their feet—making the trail look like that of a scene from a badly written horror film.

His body begged to stop, to find relief instead of pushing on, but Aura needed him. She was in danger.

The trail wound up the hillside like it had been drawn there by some sadist with a death wish. Each step was a struggle, but he moved one foot in front of another, silently hoping that he would get to her in time.

The path in the snow switch-backed. Forcing his body to climb higher, Dane came around the bend. Standing beside the horses, was Aura. Her blonde hair was disheveled, and her arm was caked in drying blood. His gun was tucked in the waistband of her jeans.

"Aura?" He rushed to her. He'd never been more relieved. He glanced down at her bloodied arms and a new fear rose within him. "Are you okay?"

His body begged to touch her, to make sure that she was really there standing in front of him—that she wasn't just some kind of apparition.

"I'm fine. What're you doing up? You shouldn't be moving," she said, sounding like an overly anxious nurse. "I didn't want to leave you, but I had to go get the horses...I was just on my way back down."

He waved her off. "Where's Ryan?" If the bastard had anything to do with hurting her, Dane would personally make sure his ass rotted in the basement of the state prison; the only light he would see would be the stars that flashed inside his head when he took another prisoner's beating.

"Ryan's fine. I just got him away from his mare. He'd fallen out the saddle when she spooked. It looks like he might have gotten dragged a little ways—his face is pretty beat up. Plus, I think he broke his nose and maybe his left ankle." She motioned to the horses. "He hasn't woken yet, I'm starting to get worried."

"He didn't touch you, did he?" Dane dropped her arm. "What happened?"

"Don't you remember?" She lifted her hand to his forehead, taking his temperature like he was a child. Her *little Danish*. "We were attacked by a wolf. The horses spooked."

He pulled back from her hand. All he had was a bump on the head, he would be fine. "Where is it?" He scanned the area looking for the beast.

"He won't be a problem again." She reached down and pulled the gun from her jeans.

Had she been hit on the head too?

"You shot the wolf with my gun?" She had to be kidding.

She shook her head. "I just don't understand it. Wolves don't normally just attack people."

"Have you read *Call of the Wild?*" He thought back to the book, in which the men huddled around the campfire as wolves circled around them. "They sure as hell do attack people."

• • •

The stunned look on Dane's face spoke more than any of his words. He must have thought she was stark raving mad—like a woman who'd spent too much time out in the Arizona sun. How could she explain to him that she could telepathically communicate with animals? Then he would think she was *really* crazy.

"I mean, I assume we were in their territory." What had she done?

Ryan moaned. A sense of relief came with the sound. Maybe Dane hadn't noticed her slip of the tongue.

She stepped around the horses, turning her back on Dane and the mistake she had made. For a cowboy, Ryan had taken the fall from the horse surprisingly hard. He'd been moaning in his sleep ever since she'd found him.

Dane stepped toward the cowboy that lay on the ground on the other side of the horses. A little droplet of blood slipped down out of Dane's hair and dripped down the side of his neck.

"Come here." Aura beckoned him with her finger. "Let me see your cut."

He touched his fingers to the blood and pulled his fingers away, smearing the trail. He looked down and grimaced. "Don't worry, I'll be fine. I just cut my head when I fell. No biggie."

"You know you don't have to be tough all the time. I want to help you. Just let me take a look."

He paused for a minute then turned his head so she could see the bloody patch of hair where his head had hit the ground. She sucked in a breath as she pulled back his hair to reveal a little jagged cut. "Are you okay?"

"I'm fine." He pulled away from her. "We need to find the bear tree. Did Ryan say how much further it was from here?"

"Before we were attacked, he said we were close. It can't be that much further now." She looked over to where Ryan lay. "But we can't leave him. And I don't think either one of you should be riding the horses."

Dane looked up at the sky. "It's getting late. Even if we started out now, we'd be trying to pack out in the dark."

Aura glanced down at her watch—it read 5:30. It would be dark in another hour. Dane was right. But what would it be like spending the night up on the mountainside with Dane and the injured Ryan?

She glanced over at Dane. She couldn't help noticing the way his pants pulled around him like groping hands. She envied the cloth.

No. She couldn't think like this. She couldn't let her nymph desires come to the surface. There was too much about this man that she liked, that she wanted to know and experience. Aura couldn't take their relationship any further than they already had. Her heart and his life would be in danger, even more than they already were.

"If we get started making a fire we could probably make it through the night," Aura said. *Unless more wolves attacked them.*

Aura followed Dane as he moved around the horses and stepped to Ryan's side.

Ryan's eyes were puffy, and the skin on the left side of his face had bad road rash. Clumps of dirt hung to his bloodied cheek, where Aura had attempted to clean, but had given up. Dane pressed his fingers against Ryan's carotid artery, checking for a pulse.

"He's alive, I already checked." She pulled her cell phone from her pocket and held it up, looking for a signal. "I tried earlier to call 911 for help, but I'm still not getting a signal."

"There must be service somewhere because we're close to where your sister last had cell service. Maybe we could keep moving up higher and try to catch a signal. Then we can call in a team to get us medevac'd out."

Aura couldn't shake the feeling of angst that crawled on her skin like a centipede, its feet tickling her nerves with warning. With Ryan unconscious, Dane hurt, and her arm injured, if they were attacked none of them could fight. They would be walking targets. She couldn't protect them. Hell, she couldn't even protect Natalie—a demi-god horse-shifter. She was useless. Tears threatened to spill over. She couldn't cry. Tears would serve no purpose, they would solve nothing. She blinked them away—she wasn't weak.

"Are you okay?" Dane stood up from Ryan's side and wiped off his knees. "Let me see." He stuck out his hand and motioned for her arm. His face was soft and caring; his gold-flecked brown eyes sparkled with unmistakable attraction. He opened his palm and motioned again.

What was happening? Who was this man standing before her? Why was he giving her *that* look? He couldn't have known that she'd saved him from the thundering horse's hooves. So why all of a sudden did he look at her like she was his? Warmth crept up her thighs, melting away her residual sense of foreboding. Maybe spending the night with Dane in the woods wouldn't be as bad as she had thought.

She extended her arm and sat it in his cupped hand, submitting to him. The heat of his skin was a shock to her chilled arm. His fingers barely touched her flesh as he pulled back the torn edges of her coat and inspected where the wolf's teeth had torn at her arm. The edges had already begun to heal and the fresh skin gleamed pink.

"Have you been bitten before?" Dane looked up at her in disbelief.

Aura pulled her arm back and tugged the shreds of her coat down over her arm. He couldn't know about her. He couldn't know who she really was; no mortal man could possibly comprehend what it meant that she was a nymph. And love was out of the question. She couldn't put anyone else in danger.

She stepped back from his overly warm touch. "I had a scar there from horse training."

He stared at her, but said nothing.

"Let's go. The top of the mountain isn't much further," she said, pointing to the trees around her with their stunted trunks that twisted from the constant bombardment of high-altitude winds.

He nodded. "Let's load Ryan and get going. We need to get him some help."

• • •

The rocks clattered down the trail, falling haphazardly as the horses moved up the mountain. Dane shouldn't have been hiking, but he refused to get back up on the horse. He cussed as one of the icy rocks slipped under his feet.

The trail switch-backed as it moved upward. To her right was a large tree, its surface marred by hundreds of scratches. Clumps of black hair stuck out from what little bark remained. They'd found the bear tree. She pulled the phone from her pocket and looked down at the screen. Two perfect little white bars glowed up at her. *Service.*

Her hands shook as she pulled the phone for Dane to see. "We need to get you guys taken care of."

"I'm fine, really. Just a little blood."

He needed to be seen by a doctor—she couldn't be responsible for Natalie's disappearance and then the two men's injuries. It was as if all she brought to anyone in her life was pain, misery, and death.

Dane ran his fingers through the back of his hair as if he was trying to cover the cut, but she'd already seen the damage she'd inflicted on him. If she hadn't brought him up here, if she hadn't let Natalie leave Arizona without her, then none of the people around her would have been in danger or hurt.

There was a tug in her chest as she glanced over to Dane. There was something about him, it could have been her nymph ways, but there was something that she simply could not resist. She desperately yearned to step to him and wrap her arms around him and never let him go. He was hers to protect.

The wind kicked up and its icy breath blew down her neck, drawing goose bumps to her skin. If she was going to protect him, the best thing she could do was to keep her heart as far away from him as possible. Danger came hand-in-hand with emotions.

She scanned the ground around them looking for some sign as she tried to ignore her ever growing feelings for Dane. Natalie was her first priority. They needed to find something, anything that could bring her sister back to her, so they could get out of this place and away from the dangers, both physical and emotional, which seemed to be around every bend.

The thick layer of ice upon the snow glistened in the cold late evening sun. A few bushes and the stunted trees were the only things that stuck out from the field of ice at the top of the mountain.

Fear filled Aura's heart. The ground had been stripped clean of any traces of her sister. Natalie was gone.

Chapter Eleven

The sun slipped over the horizon, casting long shadows over the ravines and valleys that rested around the mountain. The blades of the helicopter chopped through the air as the EMTs loaded Ryan onto a stretcher and into the bird.

One of the male life-flight nurses turned to Dane. "You sure you don't want a ride out? We can send someone for the horses."

Dane shook his head. Aura had been adamant about staying with the horses and getting them down the mountain and back to some level of safety.

"Hell of a day you picked to come up on the mountain. Didn't you hear there's another storm coming in?" The man looked at him like he'd lost his mind.

Hell, maybe he had lost his mind. He'd spent his day on the frigid peak of a mountain, looking for a woman that was more than likely dead. The shit he did in the name of a good looking woman…What was wrong with him?

Aura was sitting on a stump away from the chopper's wash; she slumped down and kept glancing over, almost as if she was afraid of the helicopter. A woman was looking at her arm. The EMT shrugged as if she too was just as confused with the state of the new wound. Aura smiled and pulled her arm back and shoved her tattered coat's sleeve down. His officer senses kicked into high gear. Something about her was just *wrong*.

"Did you hear me?" the EMT yelled.

He shook his head and looked back to the man standing at his side. "What?"

"You and your friend need to get off the mountain as soon as possible. They're giving a winter storm warning. I bet this place will get three feet of fresh snow by morning."

Any goddamned evidence that hid under the snow would be hidden until the spring now. Their odds of finding a trace of Natalie up here was as likely as his brother deciding to not be an asshole—which wasn't ever going to happen.

"We'll get down the mountain as soon as we can."

The pilot pointed toward the horizon where the sun had disappeared, but a thin line of light still permeated the evening. "You sure you can get out in the dark? I don't want to be back up tomorrow on a recovery mission where we try to find your bodies."

The man was right, it would be precarious heading back down the steep mountain trail in the dark, but he had a flashlight and blankets if they were forced to stop. He was a Montanan and a former Boy Scout—he didn't go anywhere unprepared.

"We'll be careful packing out. If we aren't out by mid-day tomorrow send in the cavalry."

The man smiled. "Will do." He motioned for the other nurse.

Dane walked over to Aura and put his hand on her shoulder. "You okay? You sure you don't want to ride out with them? I can get the horses out on my own, you know."

She glanced over at the helicopter. "There's no way I'm getting on that damned thing. At least not while I'm alive."

If they didn't get out before the storm broke it was possible that she would be getting the ride she didn't want. They needed to get moving.

He watched as the EMTs boarded the bird. The pilot gave them a thumbs-up as the bird lifted straight up off the ground, hovered, and then moved toward the North, and the nearest hospital. Aura had been right in her assumption that Ryan's leg had been broken.

From what the EMT had said, it sounded like he would need more than his fair share of pins and needles. The poor kid.

The pebbles of snow pelted his face as the copter's wash cleared away the snow on the peak. The helicopter skimmed over the next mountaintop it's lights flashed over the windswept peak. Something reflected the light, catching his attention.

Had they found something?

He moved as fast as his sore body would allow. The EMT had given him a few butterfly strips for his cut, but they hadn't done a thing for the pain that radiated up from his hips and back. The fall had been harder than he'd thought, but at least he wasn't as bad off as Ryan.

"What's that?" Aura said in an excited voice. Her footsteps crunched on the icy snow behind him as the thump of the helicopter's blades drew quieter and it disappeared from view.

On the ground, just beneath where the helicopter had landed sat a buck knife. It was folded in half, blade closed safely inside the handle. Dane stared at the handle, where he could just make out some writing.

Aura pushed past him and picked up the knife and spun it in her fingers.

"Aura, that's evidence. Fingerprints?"

She gave him a look that was sharper than the knife in her hands. "Have you looked around? There isn't a crime lab for miles. We're on our own. No one is going to magically come down and give us the person who has my sister."

In a manner of speaking she was right. It wasn't likely that there would be any trace evidence or fingerprints on the knife; at least none that hadn't already been washed away by the snow.

"Look!" Where the blade folded was a small piece of torn purple fabric. Aura pulled the fabric out of the crack in the knife and, as she opened the cloth, there was a single strand of long brown hair attached to the fabric. "Someone tried to hurt Natalie."

She lifted the hair for him to see.

"How can you be sure that this belonged to her?"

Aura lifted the cloth to her nose and took in a long breath. Her eyes darkened as she took in the cloth's scents. "This carries her smell. Whoever this knife belonged to, that's who brought Natalie to this place."

Her gaze slipped back down to the knife in her hand. "At least there is no blood." She flipped the blade over. "But wait, there are someone's initials."

He stared down at brass-plated handle of the knife where it read 'M. J. P.'

"You know anyone with those initials?"

"I don't." He thought for a second, but no one came to mind. "Do you think it's possible that Natalie was involved with someone else besides Shawn and Ryan? Maybe with a man with the initials M. J. P.?"

She pulled her arms tightly around her body, as if his question had struck some kind of nerve. "Look, my sister didn't tell me much. I guess it could have happened. But no one I know has those initials."

It was possible that they were going after a person they'd never met, never heard of, and would probably never catch—not unless the suspect made a grievous mistake. There had to be something he was missing.

"We'll figure this out." He took her chilled hand in his. "We'll find your sister. I made a promise. I intend to keep it."

If we're really lucky maybe we can even find her alive.

She stared down at their entwined fingers. Unconsciously, he leaned in, breathing in the scent of flowers, fresh air, and horses from her hair. Then one-by-one she released her fingers and drew back from him. "We just need to find who ever has those initials. Then we'll find her."

She had complained that he was tough all the time, but now here she was acting like a judge in a packed courtroom. This had to be affecting her.

Aura reached up toward him, but before her fingers touched him, her hand dropped to her side.

"Let's get out of here. It's getting dark." She spun on her heel and almost sprinted away from him.

He followed behind her and tried not to watch her ass as she walked away. Everything about her was so goddamned perfect, even her ass was perky. Why couldn't there be something about her that was less than? But no, even her boots looked good. Her butt wiggled a little too much as she moved toward the horses. Was she doing it on purpose? Was she trying to drive him mad?

The horses nickered a soft welcome as he untied them and stepped up into the saddle, holding onto Ryan's horse's lead rope. He took the front, slowly making the way down the trail, but kept looking back over his shoulder to make sure Aura was doing okay. Each time, she was looking anywhere but at him. He couldn't build up the nerve to talk, he just wanted to get out of the woods and away from the uncomfortably beautiful woman he was with. There was no way she would want to be with a man like him. She was only after one thing—Natalie. She didn't want him.

They didn't make a sound as they passed through the little stretch of trail covered in blood. There were no new fresh tracks in the snow. Hopefully that meant that there would be no more wolves.

He kept checking over his shoulder, wondering if he should say something, but there was nothing he could think of to make up for the fact that he had let her fight alone. He had let her down. She probably resented him for it. Was that why she'd pulled away from his touch?

Should he apologize? Or was he just acting stupid? It hadn't been his fault he'd gotten thrown. It could have happened to anyone, and he'd never been much of a horse guy—not even growing up on the ranch. He'd always been more of a four-wheeler guy. He hadn't meant for her to be endangered.

About half way down the mountain the snow began to fall. Big, heavy wet flakes coated the horses and blanketed the trail, making it hard to see. "Whoa," he said, pulling back the reins. He turned around. "I think it's best if we get down and hike the rest of the way."

He hated to think what would happen if one of the horses stepped on an icy patch. Dane wasn't willing to put Aura at risk more than he already had.

The horse pulled at the lead rope as he moved back to help her down out of the saddle. He moved to grab her hand, but she waved him off. "I got it."

She stepped down and ran her hands down the gelding's neck. "Shhh…It's alright, Dancer." The horse leaned into her touch, almost as he had done on the top of the mountain. Did she have the same effect on everyone?

"What are you doing? The horse is fine."

She jerked and glared at him. "He's afraid. He's not used to this type of work. This is his first time taking a rider on a trail."

"How do you know that?"

Her face softened and she looked away, but not before he noticed the guilty look on her face—a look he had plenty of experience identifying.

Aura pressed her forehead against the horse's neck. "Ryan told me. This is the horse Pat was trying to *train* when I had a falling out with your brother."

"Falling outs are easy to come by with Zeb," he said, half under his breath. "How long have you been working with horses?" He recovered, trying to bring it back to her. He needed to find out what she was hiding.

She moved away from Dancer and started down the trail. He followed behind. "I don't know. A while."

"How'd you get into working with horses?"

"I don't know," she said with an exasperated sigh, as if he was pushing too hard in trying to find out who she really was.

The horse's hooves creaked in the wet snow. "I won't stop asking questions. So it's in your best interest to start really answering them." He could play bad cop if that's what she needed. "I know you're hiding something. I won't stop until I find out what you're keeping from me."

Aura's shoulder pulled tight and her head shrank down, like she was covering her neck from attack.

"Stop."

His mare huffed next to him and Aura stopped and turned around. "What? What don't you already know about me? I like horses. I've worked with them for a long time. Forever. When I'm not training, Nat and I try to stop the BLM roundups of the wild horses. But we're not making much of a difference. I'm a goddamned failure in keeping them and my sister safe. But I'm not the one you need to be worrying about. You need to be focused on Natalie. I'm not a goddamned suspect...no matter how badly you want me to be."

"Is that what you think? That I want you to be someone I can arrest?" He stepped toward her and put his hands on her tense shoulders. "That is the last thing I want. I just want to know more...To learn who you really are."

"I'm a horse trainer from Arizona. That's it." She looked back to the horses, hiding her face.

"We both know you're lying. Why can't you just give me something? You know more about me than I know about you, and I'm not the one who needs help."

She dug the toe of her boot into the snow. Ever so slowly, she looked up. Her sapphire eyes glistened with tears. "I'm afraid, okay? I don't know how I'll survive without Natalie. She's my best friend. She's my life."

The wetness threatened to spill over and slip down her cheek. He could hardly stand it, his gut ached. Why had he pushed her for answers? He should have known that she was just worried.

He stepped toward her, careful to not drop the horse's lead rope, and pulled her into his arms. She didn't resist and she pressed her face to his chest. The warmth of her body melded with his as he breathed in her sweet scent. His body quivered to life. "I'm sorry, Aura. I didn't mean to upset you. I…I just care about you."

What had he said? What was wrong with him? Why couldn't he keep his mouth shut?

Aura leaned back and looked up at him with her shimmering sky blue eyes. "You do?"

The way she questioned him made him wonder if she'd ever heard anyone say those words to her before. The thought saddened him. Had she never been truly loved? He'd been with Angela, she'd never loved him, but she'd cared, up until …

He dropped his hands to her waist. "Of course I care about you."

Aura reached up, ran her fingers through the back of his hair, and wrapped her hands around his head. He yielded to her as she pulled him down to her lips. The soft skin of her lips tasted like honey, her sweetness melted in his mouth, filling his mouth with her flavor. What would her nipples feel like in his mouth?

His pants grew tighter as he hardened. No matter how hard he tried, he couldn't stop imagining taking her down to the ground, snow or no snow, and making love to her. Would she moan? Cry out? There was no one around, only the horses. He could make her cry out with passion and no one would hear.

She pulled at his lip, sucking gently. A groan escaped his lips and he pulled her in tighter to him, showing her what she did to him. Her hand slipped from his back and she moved back just enough to let her fingers trail down the front of his pants. The sound of his heart beating was almost deafening, the world swirled around him, and he couldn't think straight. He could only feel her hand pressing against him. The horse's lead ropes slipped from his fingers and dropped to the wet ground.

• • •

Aura mentally reprimanded herself. She shouldn't be doing this. It wasn't the right time to get involved with a man...and not just any man, but the man heading the investigation. But he was asking so many questions. For once it seemed easier to let her nymph desire take the lead.

His pulse raced under the palm of her hand as she stroked over the top of his pants. The tips of her fingers made little circles as she pulled her hand slowly upward, teasing him, making him want her more with every passing second.

She sucked softly at his full bottom lip and then let go. As a reward for the pain, she used her tongue to caress his slightly swollen lip. His tongue met hers, soft at first, but then, as if he could no longer control the hunger within him, he let his kiss hasten. He pressed his lips against her with a passion so fierce it surprised her. It was as if he feared her escape.

A snowflake fluttered down and landed on her nose, chilling her skin. She pulled back, breaking the kiss. Dane looked down at her with a lust-glazed look upon his face. His kiss-dampened lips pulled into a full smile. He reached up and softly took her face in his hands. Ever so gently, he ran his calloused thumb over the tip of her nose and wiped off the melting snow.

"I know I've said it before, but you are so goddamned sexy. I feel like I'm eighteen again." He leaned in and gave her a light kiss. He pulled back slightly, but their lips still touched. "I don't understand this...You..."

She leaned in and claimed his lips, stopping him from saying another word. She couldn't make this any more than a fling. Too much was at stake. Not only the investigation, but if he fell in love…his life would be in danger—the curse of the nymphs would strike him down. She couldn't risk the curse coming true— she couldn't love him or he would die. If she cared for him at all, this could only be a physical thing. She couldn't let her heart get involved and neither could he.

Dane let go of her face and wrapped his arms around her, hugging her close. She drew back. "If we do this, it's a one-time thing."

Rejection flickered in his eyes. "What do you mean?"

She reached up and ran her finger over his bottom lip, gently flicking his skin, not letting him forget what it felt like to kiss her. "Only once." Her fingers dropped from his lips. She ran them down the front of his jacket and to the top of his jeans.

Dane threw back his head and he moaned as her fingers weaved under his shirt and touched his hot flesh. The button flipped out of the hole and she inched the zipper down, one tooth at a time. He let go of her and moved to touch his zipper, as if she was moving too slow.

"No." She batted his hand away with a wicked smile.

He groaned and his body shifted hungrily beneath her hands. Her spell was working.

The zipper met the bottom of its trail, but she barely noticed. Dane was a boxers man. She ran her hand in between his jeans and the black cotton of his underwear. He leaned into her hand as she wrapped her fingers around him. With a confidence that came to those of her kind, she stroked him just hard enough to make him so he could be no harder, but light enough that the cloth wouldn't take away from his enjoyment.

She knelt down, letting her knees drop into the wet snow, but she didn't care.

Aura tugged at his pants, pulling them down from his hips, exposing the top of his boxers. She looked up at him. He was looking down at her with a light in his winter honey-colored eyes. His lips quivered as if he wanted to say something, but there was a need in his eyes that she was sure was reflected in her own.

His pants hung to his muscular thighs and she softly ran her fingers under the waistband of his underwear, letting her fingertip gently caress the tender flesh of his sensitive head. She pulled down his boxers, exposing him to the wintery air. Goosebumps covered his warm flesh, but that was the only indicator of the cold temps.

Taking him in her hand, she sat up and opened her mouth. "Stop. No."

What? No man had ever turned down what she was offering.

He stepped back, but she didn't let go. Dane reached down and put his hand over hers, tapping her fingers to make her let go. "Wait."

The horses nibbled at the grass that stuck out of the snow. Just to the side of the trail there was a small clearing. Pulling up his pants, he stepped to the clearing and kicked away the snow. He turned to her and smiled as he stepped to the horse and opened the saddlebag. He pulled out a red and blue striped blanket and laid it down on the ground as if setting up a picnic. "Come here."

Aura stood up and stepped over to him. She let him lay her down on the ground upon the scratchy wool blanket. He smiled down at her as he sat down on his knees beside her. She reached up for him, but this time he pushed her hands away. "No." His smile was that of a man who had a delicious plan.

He opened her jacket and slid up her shirt, exposing her belly. He moved between her legs and ran his hands over her exposed flesh, teasing her as she had mercilessly teased him. His smile disappeared as he moved to the top of her pants. Without saying a word, he unbuttoned them and pulled them free of her body.

She lay exposed, open to receive. Dane sat back and sucked in a breath as he slipped his coat off. He balled it up and laid it under her head. She was careful to not let him see the tattoo on her neck that so closely resembled that of Angela's.

Sitting back, he ran his hands down her naked thighs, making goose bumps rise to her already chilled skin. His hands moved upward, to the intersection of her thighs and over her folds. She closed her eyes as his fingers moved in agonizingly perfect circles.

His pants rustled and he slipped them off. His body moved on top of hers. She tilted her hips up and he slid inside her. She bit back a squeal of delight as he moved gently, letting her body receive him.

Reaching down, she grabbed his round, firm ass and drove him deep. The fever took over and their bodies melted into each other. Both without end, each movement met with the perfect response, as if they were of the same thoughts.

No man had ever been so good.

Dane slowed and he ran his fingers down the sensitive skin of her neck. His lips trailed up to her ear, his breath hot and wet against her earlobe. He sucked in a harsh breath and drove himself deep. A groan escaped her lips and fluttered out into the timber. He pulled back and she pushed his ass down hard again.

"Faster," she whispered in a ragged breath.

His body pounded against her, fast and hard. Stars filled her eyes and she could feel her end nearing.

He buried his face in her neck. "I'm going to come."

She nodded, but she couldn't speak. The stars in her eyes became fireworks as her body quivered and shook. Her impassioned cry penetrated the air as Dane groaned and his heat filled her.

Her breathing came in hard gasping breaths. Dane sat up and looked at her. There was a look in his eyes she could recognize, the one look she feared—love.

No...

Chapter Twelve

Zeb slammed the door to his pickup as he got out. Aura tried not to cringe as he strode out of the shadowy early morning sky and into the well-lit stables. From the look on his face, he wasn't happy to see them. "What in the hell were you two thinking?"

Aura's cheeks burned with embarrassment. It hadn't made any sense to stay out all night, but they had been so tired after they'd made love …

Dane glanced over at her and gave her a wicked grin.

"You had no business taking my horses."

"Ryan said he had your permission," Dane said, his voice in between apologetic and defensive, almost as if he wasn't sure what line he should draw with his brother.

Aura opened the stall and led Dancer in.

"That's bullshit."

She stepped back out, closed the door to the stall, and slid the lock into place. Aura turned to Zeb; she didn't want to have a fight with this man, but it seemed unavoidable. "How were we supposed to know he didn't really call you?"

"You…Well, he…" Zeb jabbed his thumb at Dane. "He should've known I would have never let him touch anything of mine."

He sounded like a spoiled child, too headstrong and selfish to share his toys.

"We needed to get to the top of the mountain. My sister has been missing for over a week. The mountain's the last place we had her cell signal. We believe whoever is behind Angela's murder might also have something to do with my sister's disappearance."

There was a flash of pain on his face, as if he suddenly remembered Angela's murder. "I'm sorry to hear about your sister. I really am, but that doesn't mean you have any business using my horses and staff to get back there."

"Don't worry about it, Zeb…we won't do anything like that again. We didn't find her and the only evidence we found—"

Dane shook his head, motioning her to stop speaking. "We only found evidence of some wolf activity up on Shirley Mountain. You had any problem with them coming down and getting into your livestock?"

Zeb stepped back, almost like he was stepping away from the fight, at least for a moment. "We lost one of the new fillies we picked up from the sale last month—we were pretty sure it was a wolf kill. You didn't see the devils, did you?"

Aura glanced over to Dane. Was he going to tell his brother the truth? Or was their distaste for each other going to taint even the investigation?

"One attacked us. We didn't see any evidence of wild game… no elk…no deer…hell, not even a squirrel track to speak of."

"They've killed everything. Now all they have left is my livestock." Zeb shook his head. "Those damn liberal environmentalists. I told Fish, Wildlife, and Parks officials about the horse, but they said to just keep an eye out for the wolves and they'd send someone out. I haven't seen hide nor hair of them. Now it has to come to this."

"Well, there's one less for you to worry about now. When it attacked us, Dancer kicked one and sent it over the cliff. That's one hell of a horse…"

Zeb stepped over to the stall and called for the horse. Dancer picked up his ears, but ignored the man's calls. He stepped back farther into the shadows of the hay-covered stall. His body told her that he hated his owner. He must have known that this was the man that had allowed Pat's mistreatment. "He's stubborn, that's for sure."

"He's upset." Aura stepped over to Zeb's side and made a clicking sound to Dancer.

The horse looked over to Zeb then back to her and then shook his head. He huffed like a boy who didn't want to obey, making Aura laugh. The horse was a special one. He had such a personality; it came through in everything he did. Dancer was strong-willed, maybe a little anti-social, but his distrust was well-justified—he was like her in so many ways.

He didn't deserve to live here, penned up in a stall most of the time, and the rest of the time having his spirit beaten down by Pat's whip. "Come here, baby. Don't worry about Zeb, he's just a—"

"Pain in the ass," Dane said, finishing her sentence.

"Hey, now." Zeb turned to face his brother. "Don't you forget for a second that I could charge both of you with theft and Aura with trespassing."

Dane's shoulders squared and he stared daggers at Zeb. "And don't forget whose wife it was that you stole…And everything I've done for you."

"Both those things were your choice."

"You think my wife cheating on me with you was my choice?"

"If you wanted her, you should have fought for her. You gave her up at the first sign of trouble. Long before I started sleeping with her."

After their moment of shared passion, Aura wanted to hear exactly what had happened between Dane and Angela. Yet, she didn't want to know…at least not like this or right now. If Dane wanted to tell her what had transpired between him and his ex-wife, he could do it in private, not prompted by his brother's narcissistic rampage.

Dancer pranced around the stall nervously as the brothers raised their voices. Dancer hated the confrontation just as much as Aura did.

"Knock it off." Aura slammed her fist down on the stall's half door. "You are brothers. Stop fighting. You are both acting like children. Besides, you're scaring Dancer."

Dancer stuck his head over the door of the stall. She ran her hand down from his soft forelock to the tip of his nose. His nostrils flared as he took in her scent. His eyes softened and he leaned into her hand as she reached around and scratched behind his ear.

"You seem so goddamned worried about that horse. Why don't you buy him from me?"

"What?" Had she heard Zeb right?

"He won't work with Pat and he's nothing but another horse to feed over the winter. I don't see why I need him."

She eyed him with distrust. "How much do you want for him?"

Zeb crossed his arms over his chest and stood silent for a moment, thinking. He eyed her like he was assessing exactly how much she was worth, and how much she would be willing to pay. "How about this…You and Dane find whoever killed Angela. When you do, I will sell him to you for five thousand."

Five thousand? She ran her hand down Dancer's neck, letting her fingers feather through his thick mane. He was worth more than five thousand as a rodeo horse, but she didn't want him for that. She wanted him as a friend, a horse that she could saddle and take on long trail rides with Natalie in her horse form at their sides.

Something about the offer struck her as fake. This was a man who loved the best things in life, from his brand new camel color boots to his pristine, fresh-off-the-lot truck—what was Zeb hiding? Did he think that they'd never solve the crime? That they'd never find the killer? Or Natalie?

She dropped her hand and turned to Zeb. "What happens if we don't find whoever is behind Natalie's disappearance?" She hated to say it. She even hated to think what would become of her if she didn't find Natalie, but she hated the thought of Pat beating the horse as well.

"Then there's no deal."

Aura stuck out her hand. "You have yourself a deal."

Zeb smiled as he took her hand and gave it a firm shake. He looked back over his shoulder to Dane. "I was going to send that little bastard to the meat auction anyway."

She dropped his hand and stepped back. The man was an asshole. How could he even be related to Dane? They seemed so different. Dane was strong, spontaneous, sweet, and caring. Zeb was strong, but in another way—almost as if his show of outer strength was only a cover for his inner weakness. Was he attempting to make up for his poor decisions by being arrogant and condescending? Was it his way of ridding himself of guilt?

What was he guilty about? Was it only his feelings of guilt for taking Angela away from Dane or was there something more? Could Zeb have had something to do with her death? With Natalie's disappearance?

If that was the case, why would he offer her a reward?

Dane suddenly pushed past her, toward the large stack of hay bales that sat at the end of the corridor. "What is this?" he growled as he pointed to the blue tarp that covered the top layer of hay.

"It's a tarp." Zeb laughed. "What's wrong with you?"

Dane picked up the end of the blue tarp up with his fingertips and stared at it for a second. He glanced up, and for a fleeting moment Aura could see something in his face. Was it anger? Or was it something else? "Why is there blood on it?"

Zeb's laughter stopped abruptly. "What are you talking about?"

"Right here." Dane pointed at a brownish spot on the plastic. His face went stoic, the Dane she'd known earlier in the night was gone, only to be replaced by the no-nonsense deputy.

Aura and Zeb rushed to Dane's side.

Zeb's face lost its color. He leaned down and stared at the spot. "That's not blood…It can't be."

"Sure as hell looks like blood to me." The blue plastic moved as Dane sat it back down on the hay. The dried blood cracked and a small fleck fell to the floor. "Before the police show up, is there anything you need to tell me, Zeb?"

"No…" His pale face turned green.

"You didn't have anything to do with Angela's death, did you?" Dane reached to his front pocket, like he was reaching for his notepad, but his fingers merely patted his jacket.

Zeb stepped back and leaned his back against the wooden wall. "I loved her, Dane…You know that."

"I never assumed you didn't. But you already admitted you were having problems. Then she shows up dead. Now this." He pointed at the blood. "It's hard to discount the evidence. So, either you had something to do with her and the other women's death and disappearance, or you know who did."

"I swear I don't know what you are talking about."

"Save your statements until you have a lawyer present." Dane pulled his cell phone from his pocket. The phone beeped as he pushed the numbers and pressed send. "Hi. This is Dane. You need to send a patrol car out to the Diamond. We have a suspect in custody."

Chapter Thirteen

The sun had started to rise over the tops of the mountains, flooding the valley and the ranch with light. The horses were getting restless in their stalls, stomping and neighing as the group of officers and investigators filtered through the stable. They hadn't found much besides the tarp, which the investigators had taken for samples and evidence.

Zeb was planted in the back seat of Officer Grant's patrol car, waiting to be taken back to the station for questioning. They could hold him for forty-eight hours before they had to let him go; which they would have to, unless he admitted having a part in the murders. There was nothing conclusive that proved Zeb was responsible. At least not until the results of the blood sample came back from the lab. If the blood proved to be from Angela or the other woman, Dane's brother would have a hard time proving that he was innocent.

There would be a lot of work to do to figure out exactly what had happened. Some things still didn't seem to fit. Zeb hadn't appeared to know anything about the second woman. Sure, he had motive and means to kill Angela, but it just didn't make sense why he'd kill two women and take a third. And if he did take Natalie, then where was she?

Dane's sergeant stepped up beside him and put his thumb in his utility belt. "Did your brother give you a confession?"

"No. Not yet."

The sergeant shuffled some of the hay on the floor with the toe of his boot. "We need to figure out who's behind all of this. The newspapers are beginning to go crazy. The *Missoulian* even made mention of a possible serial killer. It would be a real egg-on-the-face to have another murder. We can't risk what that would mean for the department. To say nothing about your standing within the county."

The man didn't need to verbalize what he was already thinking. Of course people were talking…calling them, and him, incompetent. "I'm trying to follow all the leads, Sarge. You know how this is. One step at a time."

"I'd appreciate it if you could start taking two. I even got a call from the governor this morning. We're starting to make national headlines."

Federal investigators were the last thing they needed. Sarge wasn't telling him anything he didn't already know. They needed to get this under control. And they needed to put an end to the killing.

"Hopefully we have it taken care of." Sarge gave a tight nod toward Zeb in the patrol car. "I'll push on the crime lab. See if they can get the investigation wrapped up. Maybe we can get something more from the bodies and the tarp to pin this to Zeb. That would quiet the media's talk about us if we could confirm that we have the killer in custody."

His brother was crass and tough, but did that really make him a killer? Dane couldn't come to terms with it. He and Dane had been close growing up. When they'd been boys, their dad had brought home a puppy, Charlie. It was about the cutest damn thing he'd ever seen. He and Zeb had played with it all day long, running around the fields, throwing sticks for him, and letting him swim in the creek that twisted through the ranch. At night, like any ranch dog, their dad made Charlie stay outside in a little doghouse he'd built.

One night, Dane had woken up to the dog yelping and screaming with pain. Zeb had been the first one out the door, carrying his little .22 caliber rifle. There, outside of the doghouse, two coyotes had attacked the puppy, tearing at him like he was nothing more than a chicken. When Zeb finished shooting, the coyotes lay dead in the yard, but Charlie was saved. Zeb had wrapped the dog in his coat and carried the little pup inside. He'd spent every minute with that dog, nursing him back to health.

Zeb couldn't be a killer. He was just a rancher and a man, who'd, in the past, wanted the best for his animals.

But then again, he'd let Pat beat that damned horse in front of Aura. Had he changed? Was he capable of killing Angela?

"We'll get this figured out," Dane said. "I'll make sure the real killer comes to justice."

Sarge's eyebrows rose. "You don't think it's Zeb? He's not a real saint, you know."

"I'm more than aware." Had the sergeant forgotten what had transpired between him and Zeb? They were brothers, but they'd never again be friends. Not since their father's death and everything that had gone on with Angela.

Aura pushed past an officer who was knelt down by the door, pushing through the hay that littered the floor.

"Where do you think you're going?" Dane called after her.

She kept walking. "I'm not done with him yet."

Sarge glanced over to him. "She seems like your kind of woman. Won't take shit from anybody."

The man kneeling down by the door laughed, but Dane didn't see anything funny.

"Why don't you just worry about watching out for horse shit?"

The man's smirk disappeared. Dane smiled as he jogged out the door after Aura.

She threw open the door of the patrol car and thrust her phone in Zeb's face. "Do you know Natalie? Have you seen her?"

Zeb looked down at the screen. The rancher's eyes widened and his mouth opened like he wanted to say something.

"Please, if you have, tell me. I just want to find her." There was a desperate edge to her voice that made Dane's skin prickle. He'd been on so many cases throughout the years, but there was something about this one that was different. All families were desperate to help their loved one, to find answers, but it was as if Aura's life was on the line, not just Natalie's.

"Answer me!" She jabbed the phone at him.

Zeb twisted in the seat, readjusting his handcuffs. "There was a guy here last week." He squirmed as he was talking, as if he was trying to think of lies as he spoke. "The guy said he needed a job. That woman, your sister, was with him. But I think they said they were headed back to Arizona or something."

Dane walked to the door and leaned over the top, looking down on Zeb. "Wait. You saw her? She was still alive?"

Aura looked up at him like he was guilty of some crime just because he'd let his thoughts slip out. She couldn't have thought Natalie was alive. Especially since they'd found the blood-covered shirt and her deserted pickup. And hell, as much as he'd like to hope, there was nothing to say that she was still alive *now*. A lot of things could have happened in the last week. It only took a second to take a life.

"The last time I saw her she was," Zeb said. "But like I said, they mentioned they were leaving Montana."

"Who was the man she was with?"

"His name was Shawn something…I don't know much about him. I guess I'd seen him around town before…maybe at the ranch store. I can't really recall."

Aura gasped. "Shawn was the man from the video…"

Dane reached over the top of the car door and took her hand. "Don't worry, sweetheart. We'll find Shawn. We'll find her."

The news of the murders had hit the town and the papers. If Shawn had anything to do with the murders he would be hiding out. Where would they be? If he were a man on the run, where would he hide? Or had Zeb been telling the truth? Had they left the state?

"Zeb, another officer will meet you at the station and will have some questions for you. I'll make sure to let them know that you've been helpful."

No matter what had happened between them in the past, Zeb was still his only brother. And no matter how much evidence pinned him to the murders and disappearance, Dane simply couldn't swallow the fact that Zeb was capable of killing his wife or anyone else. Yet, he was a sheriff's deputy and he had to follow the letter of the law. He would do his best to protect his brother, but he needed to do his job and follow all the leads wherever they led him. Time would tell whether or not his brother was guilty of any crimes.

"Thanks." Zeb relaxed into the plastic seat and laid his head back.

"And hey, Zeb, I'll try to contact the crime lab and see if they have anything more about the cause of death."

"Just so you know, I didn't have anything to do with Angela's death. And as much as you don't want to hear about it, I loved her. I don't know what I'm going to do without her."

It had been a long time since his brother had been so candid... so honest and it made his suspicion grow. Zeb was lying about something—but what?

"I know, Zeb. I know you loved her." He slowly pushed the door closed. "I loved her too." *She just never felt the same for me.*

The door clicked shut.

"Are you okay?" Aura looked at him—in her eyes there was a look of honest concern, almost as if she could sense his wavering emotions.

"I think I just need some sleep and to get away from the ranch." There were just too many memories that wanted to elbow their way into his mind. He kept trying to push away the thoughts of them as kids, his mother and father, and the night he'd found Angela in Zeb's arms.

"What about the barn? Has anyone looked in there for any evidence? Did they find anything?"

"Honey, it's okay. They have the investigation under control."

"Did *you* check the barn?"

How could he tell her that he would never enter that place? That there were things on this ranch that haunted him to this day, and every cell in his body wanted to get off the land and away from his memories. No matter how much concern she had for him, she wouldn't understand.

"They've got it, Aura."

She glanced back at the stables. "Why don't you just take me back to my truck at the main house and then I'll go to the campsite?"

So much had happened in the last twenty-four hours. He'd almost forgotten that they'd met here only with the intention of talking to Zeb about gaining access to the land. And there was still so much work to do.

"I'll take you back to your truck."

She nodded and pulled her torn coat down over her hands. Her face was drawn and tired. She'd had one hell of a day. He should have taken her back sooner, but he'd been so wrapped up in it all.

"How's your arm?" Before she could stop him, he took her hand and pushed back her sleeve.

She jerked in his hands, but he held tight. The skin of her arm was pink and tight like a fresh scar, but there was nothing else. The teeth marks that had been bleeding on her arm only a few hours before were gone.

His breath left him like he'd been punched in the gut. "What the fuck?" He dropped her arm.

Aura glanced back over her shoulder. "Shhh." She drew her finger to her mouth, motioning him to keep quiet. "We need to talk."

. . .

Dane had begrudgingly given Aura his address, along with a promise to listen to everything she had to say. A knot of dread tightened in her stomach. Was she really ready to tell him everything? Everything about her and Natalie? Undoubtedly, he was going to freak out. He probably wouldn't even believe her. He'd probably try to have her committed to a psych ward.

In her long life, she'd never told a man the truth of her condition. For the last few hundred years she had avoided any emotional entanglement. She'd lived a little hard, moving from one place to another, avoiding anything beyond short term relationships with men. But it used to be different. Marriage wasn't always about love. It was most often nothing more than a business arrangement in which the man was the patriarch and the woman was forced into the subservient role. In the early days of the United States, this type of patriarchal society required that she had a man in her life. And whenever the women of the community found out she wasn't married, questions of her capabilities as a woman always arose.

That's how'd they'd found their way to Arizona. The desert had offered them something no place else ever had—in Yuma they had found a safe haven from humanity and a place amongst the wild horses that roamed the plains. Natalie had loved it. It was where she had completely embraced everything she was—horse, woman, and nymph.

It had been wonderful until the roundup of the wild mustangs by the Bureau of Land Management starting in the 1950s. Then even their safe haven had turned into hell on earth. The sound of hundreds of hooves pounding against the dry earth, the scream of frightened horses, and the yelling of men filled her memory. She shuddered and tried to blink away the image. She couldn't think of the wounds of her past.

After a hot bath and less than a restful night, the next morning Aura pulled the truck down the road that matched the directions Dane had given her to his home. At the end of the short street sat a ruddy pine-colored house. Its windows were closed and the blinds were pulled shut, shielding Dane from the outside world. The yard was covered in snow, but the driveway had been shoveled in a perfect pattern and not a single extra bit of snow was out of place.

There were no decorations on the outside of the house except an aged, sun-bleached *Welcome* sign that had been put up beside the front door. It wasn't hard to tell that the sign was a remnant from the days of Angela. A profound sense of sadness filled her. He had gone through so much that would have ruined most men, or at the least, left them closed to emotions. Yet he'd opened up to her and given part of himself to her. And she'd have to break his heart.

She knocked on his door, still not knowing what she was going to say. She tried not to think about the horrible things that could go wrong. He didn't seem like the type of man who would hurt her; he loved helping people too much. But she couldn't even guess how he'd respond. That was, if she told him the truth. Was there a way she could avoid telling him who she really was?

The sound of his footsteps grew closer and she stepped back and waited for the door to open. The footsteps stopped behind the door. It was silent for a moment. She waited.

If he didn't let her in, she could understand. She was a freak of nature. A cursed monster. He didn't need her or her mess in his life. She turned and stepped off the porch.

He may not have needed her, but she needed him. Aura turned back. "Dane, let me in. Please."

The lock clicked open and the knob turned. He slowly pulled the door open. Dane was staring at the floor like he couldn't stand the sight of her. Her heart lurched in her chest with the thought.

"Can't you look at me?" There was an edge of desperation and disbelief to her voice.

He looked up. "Hey. I'm sorry. I'm just tired."

His face was pale and his eyes were bloodshot, but he was lying. Just because he was tired didn't explain why he hadn't wanted to answer the door.

"You can be honest. You just didn't want to talk to me." She grabbed the door. "That's fine. You can just listen." She slammed the door behind her as she walked into his living room.

The place was a bit barren. A single chair sat right in front of a giant television. Against the far wall was a couch with a glass end table covered in outdoor and ammo magazines. She walked over to the couch and sat down.

Dane's cell phone vibrated on the counter and a rock song filled the tense air between them. He looked over toward the phone like he wanted to run to answer it...anything to avoid what was happening between them.

"Why don't you answer it?" she said, pointing at the phone. It would give her a moment to collect her thoughts.

Dane walked over to the small kitchen that connected it to the dining room and picked up the phone. "Hello?"

A woman's shrill voice sounded from the phone, but Aura couldn't hear exactly what she was saying, only the muffled tones. The two talked for about a minute, but Dane mostly nodded or used the typical male responses of "yeahs" and "uh-huhs."

A strange flicker of jealousy fluttered through Aura. Who was the woman who would be calling him? She tried to push the feelings aside. He was a deputy, a civil servant. He talked to hundreds of women on a daily basis and he was probably around more than his fair share of women who were willing to give him everything they had to get out of a ticket or just to get a chance to fulfill a fantasy.

She ran her fingers over the edge of the couch cushion. She had no right to feel anything about what he did or didn't do. She had told him it was only going to be a one-time thing. And though they had made love, he wasn't hers. He'd made her no promises. And he shouldn't. Dane couldn't be hers. Not if he wanted something more than a romp in the woods.

"Okay," Dane answered. "Thanks for calling." He sat the phone down on the counter and slowly turned to her. "That was the medical examiner. They got the rest of the lab work back." His face was even paler than it had been when she'd arrived and his eyes more tired.

"What did she say?"

"The blood on the tarp was equine. So they couldn't hold Zeb."

"Did they find out anything about the women?"

"There was no clear evidence as for cause of death, but both women were missing large chunks of hair at the base of the heads." He shook his head. "They each had clear defense wounds on their arms and there was some bruising on and around their abdomens."

"Did they find out anything more about the green and yellow fibers? Where they came from?"

Dane shook his head. "She thinks it was from a type of rope, but it's a rope that is sold in about every store. So it's not of much use unless we find something that would match the description."

He walked over and dropped onto the couch next to her. Nervously, he ran his hands down and over his knees and then glanced up at her. "Your sister wasn't pregnant, was she?"

"*What?*" She fast-forwarded through her memories. No. A nymph couldn't become pregnant, could they? "No. Natalie couldn't have children."

"Are you sure?"

"There's no way." At least, she didn't think so …

"Both women killed had high levels of gonadotropins in their bodies. It turns out they were taking the fertility drug Clomiphene.

They must have been trying to get pregnant. I didn't know that Angela had wanted children..."

The sadness in his voice made chills run down her spine. "I'm so sorry, Dane." She leaned over to him and wrapped her arms around him, pulling him into her chest. He resisted for a second, and then let his body relax into hers.

His arms moved around her and he burrowed his face into her neck. His breath warmed her as his full lips grazed over her neck. His kisses ran up her neck and he tugged at her earlobe gently with his teeth. She struggled to hold back a moan. It felt so good to have him in her arms, wanting her, but now wasn't the time. He couldn't stall dealing with his emotions, it wasn't healthy. They needed to talk.

She softly pushed him back from her. "Dane?" she whispered.

"Hmm?" His eyes were filled with lust. He reached over and unzipped her coat. Aura let him slip it off her shoulders. He dropped it on the floor.

"How do you know Angela wanted a baby? What if someone else was giving her the meds?"

"What?" The question must have pulled him from his haze. "Wait...You could be right." He looked stunned at the revelation.

"Do you think this could have had something to do with why they were killed?" She shuddered at the thought. "Do you think whoever did this wanted them to get pregnant?"

"It's possible, but it's hard to say. I guess it would make sense. But if your sister is still there and taking these meds..." He stared at her as he refused to say what he was thinking.

"She's being raped," she finished his sentence. Nausea engrossed her and she ran to the kitchen. She made it to the sink just in time.

Dane stepped behind her and rubbed her back. "For all we know, that might not be what's going on. And she had to tell them that she couldn't get pregnant. Maybe they are using her for something—" He clipped his sentence short as he must have realized that he wasn't making anything better.

A fresh wave of sickness overtook her. She heaved again. Her back shook as she tried to control the sickness. Natalie was strong, but she didn't deserve to be a prisoner, to be used for unspeakable things. It couldn't be. Not her sister.

He was quiet as he ran his hand up and down her back, trying to comfort her—but it wasn't working. "Who knows what was really going on? Angela wasn't known for her ability to stay with a single man. Maybe she wanted to have kids. Maybe she got wrapped in something weird."

Dane stopped rubbing. Opening a cabinet, he grabbed a glass and filled it with a bit of water. "Here," he said, sitting the glass at the edge of the sink.

Aura needed to be strong. She stood up too fast and the world swirled around her. She grabbed the edge of the sink, waiting until the light-headedness passed.

"Are you okay?"

Aura nodded, but she felt anything but fine. Her sister was missing and women were dead. *May the gods be with Natalie.*

She picked up the glass and took a sip and swirled it around, washing away the bitter taste in her mouth. When she was done, she sat the glass down, turned on the water, and washed out the sink. Dane didn't need to see her this way. She needed to keep her distance, both emotionally and physically. Natalie needed her even more than she'd first thought. A new sense of urgency filled her. If Natalie was still alive, the gods only knew what atrocious things were happening to her. Aura's imagination filled with thoughts she shuddered to even acknowledge.

Using a paper towel she wiped her face and tried to swallow away the residual feelings of sickness. She wasn't helping anything. "Where's your garbage?"

He pointed under the sink. Opening the door she threw the towel away and turned to face him. "We need to find Shawn. He'll lead us to Natalie."

"We put out an APB on his truck, but nothing has come in yet. At least nothing I've heard."

"We can't sit here and do nothing. We need to get out there and find her. Now."

"We don't know for sure that Shawn had anything to do with this."

She hugged her arms around her. "Zeb said he'd seen Shawn around. He was in the video…"

"But he doesn't have the initials M. J. P. He couldn't be responsible for the women's deaths and Natalie's kidnapping."

"There's no reason to believe he didn't. He could have stolen that knife."

"Aura," he said, touching her arm like he was talking to a stubborn child. "Just because he's in the video and they were fighting doesn't mean he's the man we are after. He very well could be, but as you know, we believe in due process and everyone is innocent until proven guilty. Even if we find him, without a confession we'll have nothing to pin him to the murders."

"I know, but how can we find evidence that ties him to the murders and my sister by standing around here?" She pushed off from the sink and walked out to the living room. She pulled on her coat and strode to the door.

Dane moved in front of her, blocking the door. "Where are you going? I thought we were going to talk?"

"Talking can wait. My sister needs me." She reached around him and took the door handle. "Now, you can come with me, or you can sit in here and do nothing. Either way, I'm going to find her."

"Wait." Dane stepped away from the door and grabbed his utility belt and black uniform jacket that hung in the side closet. "I'm going with you."

Chapter Fourteen

Del's Bar was a shit-hole by anyone's standards. The bar stunk of old tobacco, stale beer, and vomit. The floor was covered in wood shavings that they must have used to try and mask some of the rank odors, but even the fresh shavings did nothing to help. A man was standing behind the bar. He had a crooked nose and a receding hairline. What little hair he had left was gray and grease laden.

A few men stood at the far end of the bar playing pool. Another man and woman sat at the poker machines, gambling away their money. None of them made eye contact as Dane strode to the bar and pulled out a stool for Aura to sit down. She slid into the seat and then he sat down next to her and turned to the bartender.

"I'll have a beer. What do you want, honey?" There was a foreign ownership in his own voice that surprised him. Where had that come from?

He watched her pink lips twitch as she ordered a beer. He wanted to kiss those lips again, but for now he just wanted to keep her safe. The bartender looked at her. "Which one?"

Aura glanced to him questioningly, as if she wasn't much of a drinker.

There was a lot that could be assumed about a man by the beer he drank—especially at a bar like Del's. The man eyeballed them, waiting for them to decide so he could finish sizing them up. The uniform mustn't have been enough for the man to dislike him, so Dane held out a hope that there was a possibility of getting some answers.

"We'll take two draft Bud Lights." He was normally a lager drinker, but this type of situation called for a low-key American beer. Something that showed they were simple, straight to the point, and not here for any bullshit.

The man grabbed a couple of pint glasses and put them under the tap.

"You here to bust us for something?" He pushed the second glass under the tap. "We've been carding all the young-looking kids that come in this joint. We ain't done nothing illegal."

Of course the man would think a deputy would be coming here to deliver tickets, but they were here for something better—answers. "You aren't in any trouble. Just wanted to stop by, have a beer."

The man slid the beers over the bar to them as he gave them the stink eye. Dane couldn't blame the guy for not believing him. He'd never set foot in this bar unless it had been to apprehend a criminal or bust up a fight. The bartender had every reason to be suspicious.

Dane pulled out his wallet and laid a fifty dollar bill on the bar. "We are here for a little information. We just need to get you to take a look at a picture for us." He pulled Natalie's phone out of his pocket and pulled up the picture of Shawn. "You recognize this guy?"

The bartender set to washing a used pint glass, but leaned over far enough to see the picture. He acted like he was only half interested, but it was easy to tell the guy was chomping at the bit to get some fresh gossip in the place. Nothing would make a better story for later in the night than a sheriff coming in looking for a suspect.

Dane pulled back the phone, like he was reeling in a fish. The man leaned over further, taking the bait. Nothing worked like using a person's curiosity to get him to talk.

"We just need a little information about this guy. What he's driving. Who he's been with…"

The bartender stared at the screen. "I think I've seen the guy. Don't know his name, but he was in here with a pretty little brunette number."

"When was that?"

"I don't know…three or four days ago." The guy leaned back and wiped his hands on the rag at his waist.

"Was Natalie—I mean *the woman* upset?" Aura looked anxious as she leaned over the bar after the man, almost appearing as if she was going to reach out and grab him to keep him from moving away. She had a lot to learn about interrogation.

"She didn't talk much…I don't really remember her." He thought for a minute. "She was cute, I guess. Had a couple of guys giving her everything they had to get a chance to be alone with her. She stuck to that guy pretty good though." He motioned to the phone.

Did Natalie want to be with Shawn? Had they gotten it all wrong? Was she just hiding from her sister? No…There were dead women to be accounted for. But maybe, just maybe, Natalie wasn't as innocent as Aura had been putting on.

"Did you see what the guy was driving?"

The man eyed the fifty dollar bill. "My memory is a little foggy."

Dane pulled out his wallet and pulled out another fifty. If this was how the questioning was going to keep going he'd need to find a sponsor.

"Silver GMC, Idaho plates."

"Idaho? You sure?"

The man nodded and turned to put a glass away. "Positive. Saw it when I was running a load of trash out. He and that woman were having a good time in the front seat."

Aura blanched, but tried to cover her horror by taking a long swig from the heady beer.

"By chance did you catch the woman's name?"

The guy stood still for a moment, as if he couldn't think and work at the same time. "I don't know it might have been Brenna or Jenny. Something like that. Maybe."

At least he hadn't said Natalie. Not that he took any comfort in the bullshit names he had provided.

"Did you hear any mention of where they were staying?"

"I don't know about that." The bartender eyed the room to make sure no one was watching. When it seemed like no one was paying attention, he picked up the money on the bar and stuffed it into his pocket. "There was another guy with them though. Older guy. I've seen him around here before, but he didn't look real happy to be here with them. He kept trying to leave and your guy kept stopping him. They were fighting about some stock auction…Something about some wild horses they had, but that's about all I know."

At least he wasn't going to have to give the man any more money to get answers and they had gotten a few questions answered.

Dane took a long drink of his beer and wiped the foam from his lip. "Thanks for the information." He pulled a business card from his pocket with a picture of a badge and his number in bold black print. "If you see him, the other man, or the girl, I'd appreciate it if you'd give me a call. We need them to answer some questions for us."

"This about those two dead chicks?"

So much for secrets. Everyone knew what he was up to. If he didn't find answers soon his ass would be on the line.

"Like I said, just need them to answer a few questions for us."

The man smirked and walked to the other end of the bar where a barfly waved him down.

Aura turned to him. "Natalie hated Shawn…It couldn't have been her in that car with him."

She could be right, but from what the bartender said, her sister had been a willing participant in the late night romp.

"Was there any reason your sister wouldn't want to speak to you?"

She nibbled at her lip and she stared down at her beer. After a minute she looked up. "We'd had a fight, but she wouldn't just disappear."

"Not even if she had something to do with Angela's murder?" He hated that he had to ask her, but the truth needed to be found. He needed the real answers.

"She's not a killer. There's no way."

He twisted the beer in his hands. "Aura, you need to tell me what is going on. You are lying to me...I can feel it. If you care for me at all you need to tell me what the hell you're hiding."

The sound of pool balls being racked echoed across the room, making the silence between them that much more tense.

Didn't she care for him at all? If she did, she would tell him the truth—hell, she already would have.

She didn't give a shit about him. She didn't give a shit about anyone except her damn sister.

He swallowed the last drink of his beer. The glass slammed down on the bar as he stood up. "I'll be outside."

She didn't stop him.

He pushed open the door and headed out toward the patrol car. He needed to get his mind back on work. He'd been a fool to think that she wanted anything more from him than a quickie. She was using him to find her sister. If nothing else, it was damn smart of her...give an officer a little ego boost, a little sheet time, and then manipulate him to get whatever it was she wanted. How had he been taken for such a ride?

The door closed behind him. He shoved his hands into his pockets and put his head down into the freezing wind. He was sick of this place. This life. Maybe he would have been better off staying at the ranch…No. Dane shook off the thought. He should have never stayed in this God-forsaken little town. He should've joined the Army, run away to another country and done some real good.

Cars buzzed by on the highway that ran outside the bar. As Dane pushed the unlock button on the key fob, a truck pulled into the space next to him. Behind the wheel was Zeb, and from the pucker on his face, it was more than clear that he wasn't too happy to be seeing his arresting officer and brother standing next to his truck.

Zeb pushed open his truck's door and stepped out, slamming the door behind him. "What the hell? Can't a guy even get a drink without you being around?

"Look, I was only here to have a drink." He twisted the keys in his hands as he tried to think of a way to deescalate his brother's anger. "Hey man, I'm sorry I had to arrest you. It's the policy. If you want, I'll buy you a beer…to make up for it."

"I'm your goddamned brother. I don't care if it's procedure or not. You know I'm not the one behind the murders. I could never do shit like that. Yet you couldn't just live and let live. You had to go after me for Angela…and the ranch. You need to let shit go."

"I need to let shit go?" Dane's anger threatened to boil over. "You are the one standing there blowing up at me. I offered to buy you a goddamned beer. Thought we could just move past this."

Zeb pulled a can of snuff from his pocket and pushed a pinch full into his mouth and under his bottom lip. "You don't know what you cost me."

"You have all the money you need thanks to the ranch. You're full of it."

"Money's not the issue."

He wasn't making any sense. What could be more important to his brother than money? "What are you talking about?"

"It's none of your goddamned business."

"You're making it my business. Tell me what the hell you are talking about."

"What is it about you? Do you just want to live up my ass? You've been nothing but a pain in my ass ever since that Aura woman showed up around here. Fuck her and get it over with."

He refused to take the bait. He wasn't about to fight about Aura. "I bet there's not much room in your ass—not with your head so far up it."

Zeb spat on the ground. "You think you're real fucking smart, don't you? I know you only arrested me to satisfy some asshole urge...you've always been jealous of me. Of what I had. Who I am."

"You can go fuck yourself. The last person I'd want to be is you. You're a pile of shit."

"This has been a long time coming." Zeb rushed toward him, throwing his cowboy hat on the ground.

Dane dropped his shoulder, covering his head as Zeb swung his fist wildly through the air. His hand whooshed past his head, missing him by a few good inches. Dane stood back up, fists raised.

Zeb swung again.

Dane smiled wickedly. "You fight like a woman."

"You didn't use to say that. You used to get your ass beat and then cry like a little bitch."

He could envision his fist connecting with his brother's square jaw. He could feel the way his knuckles cracked across his jaw... But he stopped himself. No matter how badly he wanted to pummel the asshole he couldn't. He was wearing a uniform that stood for honor and justice...not for settling longstanding family feuds.

The bar door swung open and Aura came running out. "What the hell do you think you two are doing?"

Dane turned toward the noise.

He never saw the punch coming.

Chapter Fifteen

What was wrong with men that made them think fighting was always the answer?

Aura dabbed the wet rag over Dane's forehead, wiping away a little speckle of blood that had risen from the cut above his eye, matching the little cut in his hair. His eyes fluttered a bit as he must have felt the cold cloth on his head, but he didn't wake up.

Zeb sat at the bar drinking a beer, but he kept glancing over his shoulder almost as if checking to see if Dane was okay. Aura tried to assume that it was out of mere concern, but she couldn't shake the feeling that he was more worried about the consequences of assaulting a police officer.

She just didn't understand that man…Dane was more tolerant of him than he should have been and yet the man kept trying to set him off. It was a wonder Dane hadn't taken the chance to punch him in the face. A tendril of guilt wiggled up her spine. She was the reason he was lying here in the tacky red vinyl booth. If she would have just given him the answers—or at least some of the details—he would have never charged out of the bar and straight into a fight.

"Dane?" She shook his shoulder slightly.

His eyes fluttered, but he kept them closed.

Maybe he needed to go to the hospital. He had been out for over five minutes and Zeb had been forced to help carry him into the bar. His head had hit the concrete hard, but Zeb had convinced her to give Dane a minute to recover…that "he'd be alright."

She pulled her phone out of her purse and it reminded her of Natalie. If Dane was in the hospital, the department would assign someone else to the case and she would have to start at ground zero. But if Dane was hurt, he needed to see a doctor. He needed to be safe and taken care of, and maybe the best way was for him to be as far away from her as possible.

Aura ran her fingers through his chestnut hair. It was so full and lush; he would age well. Whoever had the opportunity to spend their life with him would be a lucky woman. He was handsome, smart, ambitious, and he lived his life with a morality that rivaled Mother Theresa. Everything he did seemed to be with honorable intentions. He was a saint. Almost. In the woods he'd been anything but saintly—he'd been carnally voracious.

She wiggled in the seat as she thought about him between her thighs. He'd taken her to a place few men had. The tender flesh at her center warmed as she remembered how he'd grazed his lips over her flesh, up her chest, and then sucked on her nipples. She wanted to feel that, and him, again.

Leaning down, she traced her fingers over the fine lines that surrounded his eyes, down over the dark stubble upon his cheeks. She feathered her finger over the skin of his lips. They were slightly chapped from the cold and she tried to remember exactly how they'd felt against her lips. She couldn't remember …

Though she lifted her finger and ran it over her lips, the feeling wasn't the same. It wasn't his kiss. No one was watching. Zeb was chatting with the bartender and the other people in the bar were stuck in their own worlds. There would be no one to judge her, or him.

When her lips touched his, he jerked beneath her as if he felt the energy that flowed between their touching mouths. She closed her eyes and ran her hand through his locks. The kiss lasted longer than she'd wanted, but she couldn't bring herself to pull away from his lips. This could be their last kiss.

A hand caressed her cheek and her eyes snapped open. Dane was looking up at her. She pulled back from the kiss.

"I'm…sorry." Her cheeks flames with lust and embarrassment. "I thought you were…"

"Dead?" he said with a weak chuckle.

"I was just about to call an ambulance."

"No need. I'm right as the rain." He moved to sit up, but fell back down to her lap.

"I can see that." She lifted his head and sat it down on her other arm, to cradle his head.

He smiled up at her. There was something unfamiliar in the way he looked at her and for once she wished she could know what he was thinking. He didn't look upset or angry. He looked almost as if he…loved her.

She picked up the rag and dabbed at his eye a little too hard.

"Ouch." He jerked.

"You had a little bit of blood." She pointed above her eye. "Just there."

He grabbed a hold of the table's edge and pulled himself to sitting. "I think I need to apologize for the way I acted at the bar. I shouldn't have run out on you like I did."

"It's alright." A sense of guilt rose up within her, but she tried to ignore the feeling. She had to protect him, even if it meant not telling him the full truth.

"Has anyone ever told you you're not great at opening up?"

She chuckled. "Well, has anyone ever told you that you need to learn to fight?"

A little color returned to his pale face. "Every man needs to take a punch for the woman he cares about. Builds character."

She squirmed in her seat. She had been right about the look in his eyes—at least a bit. He said *cared*. To think that he loved her would be presumptuous. Wouldn't it? She glanced over at him and met his gaze. There was a fire in his earthy brown eyes. She could only hope it wasn't love that had ignited the flames.

The door to the bar flew open and banged against the wall as Pat strode into the bar. His cowboy hat was low on his face, covering his eyes. He seemed not to notice her or Dane as he sat down at the bar next to Zeb.

Dane stared over at the men and he put his finger to his lip as he motioned for her to stay silent. She nodded and strained to hear the talk of the two men above the noise of the bar.

Pat waved at the bartender and waited as the man poured him a beer. "The sale went real good. I think I got some buyers lined up."

"Did you take care of our *little problem*?" Zeb glanced back at them and Aura tried to play off that she was rifling through her purse.

Pat followed his gaze. "Son of a bitch. What are *they* doing here?"

She couldn't hear what Zeb said, but Pat nodded and turned his back to them. The bartender slid a beer in front of Pat. Zeb said something she couldn't hear. The bartender looked over to them and then turned and flipped on a black stereo that sat perched on the back counter. A country song by George Strait filled the bar and covered the voices of the men.

"What sale are they talking about?" Aura asked.

Dane turned to her. "My brother likes to buy wild horses. He breaks some and then sells others to be used as rodeo stock."

Her stomach tied into a tight knot. "He does what?"

"You know…wild horses…Mustangs. The BLM rounds them up, sells the healthy ones at auctions. He picks them up for cheap, then turns around and sells them for a quick profit."

"He wouldn't…" Her body went numb. She'd never been this close to anyone that had bought a wild horse. Was this how

Natalie had gotten so wrapped up with these men? Was that why she had lied?

"Excuse me." She stood up and made her way to the restroom.

Dane looked at her like she was crazy, but she didn't care. She needed to get away just for a second. Get her head straight. Come back to center. They hadn't found Natalie. And if she had to bet, Zeb was behind her disappearance. It couldn't be just a coincidence that they fought against the roundups and the men who profited from them, and Zeb had been in contact with her. Natalie was never short on opinions, and if she knew what Zeb had been doing she wouldn't have missed the chance to tell him what she thought.

The door to the bathroom swung open and revealed a cracked sink that hung crooked on the wall. Next to the door were a dented condom machine and a broken paper towel dispenser.

She stepped to the sink and stared into the mirror. The yellow light above her cast shadows around her eyes and made her skin seem the color of dirty snow. On the wall behind her someone had scrawled a phone number. She tried not to think of the things that went on in this room, the stupid choices, and lousy mistakes. She hated everything about this bar, from the way it smelled of cheap booze to the men sitting at the bar.

She wanted to rush out into the bar and break Zeb's neck. He had something to do with what was going on and he needed to pay. But there had to be a better way to take him down. What was she going to do?

Her head pounded with the start of a headache. What had Natalie gotten herself into?

She turned on the faucet and splashed her face with cold water.

Zeb sat out there full of self-righteous pride, thinking he'd been wronged for being arrested. He deserved to sit in prison. Anyone who trafficked in wild horses deserved to be behind bars.

Bile burned her throat and her mouth turned bitter. She'd fought for so long to stop the culling of the wild herds. She and Natalie had worked so hard…and in front of her was the man who profited from thwarting her in her efforts to stop the travesty that was the roundups. Wild horses deserved to be wild, not enslaved and beaten by money-hungry tyrants.

She washed out her mouth.

Maybe she could seduce him and find out where Natalie was that way. But what would Dane think? She couldn't do it while he was around or he may never forgive her. Even though they couldn't have a future together, she didn't need to destroy the precious little time that they would have together.

There had to be a way to get what she needed. And maybe she could stop him from sponsoring the slaughter of innocent animals.

She closed her eyes and long-buried memories flooded her mind. It had to have been in the early 1900s. The herd they'd been running with that morning had meandered down dusty stagecoach tracks. The black stallion with the white blaze face had led them down the red scrub brush hillside to a small oasis. At its center sat a blue watering hole.

The alpha mare, a beautiful paint, stepped beside the stallion and took a long drink and was quickly followed by the rest of the herd. Aura could still remember the scent of bitter almonds. At the time her mouth had watered with hunger from the smell, but now it only made the burn of the acid in her throat more severe.

Aura waited her turn to get around the tiny hole, munching on the patch of green grass that grew around the little pond. Before she had the chance to reach the edge of the water, the alpha mare lay dying and Natalie lay sick on the bank. It had taken years for her beautiful sister to fully regain her health. If she had been a normal wild mustang she would have surely died like thousands of others.

She blinked back her tears.

The BLM used the helicopter roundups as an alternative to the antiquated way of eradicating the wild horses from fertile grazing grounds—ground the ranchers had wanted for their cattle. It was better than euthanizing them with cyanide, but many still died.

Modern day ranchers, for the most part, would never think of murdering horses, but by allowing the roundups and supporting them in the way they were advocating abuse. Zeb was a monster.

She had to fight him the only way she could. She would find the evidence and pin him down to the murders. He could spend the rest of his life behind bars.

The door creaked as she opened it and stepped out into the stale air of the bar. Zeb and Pat were gone.

Parked outside was another sheriff's car. She stepped out of the narrow hall and there, sitting across from the table from Dane, was another officer. He had his fingers tented in front of his stoic face. He said something she couldn't hear. Dane dropped his head into his hands.

The officer looked up and, noticing her, said something to Dane. Dane turned and stared at her. His eyes were red and bloodshot.

What had happened?

She rushed to the table. "What's going on? Did you find Natalie?"

The man looked at Dane like he wanted him to be the fall guy so if she went crazy he wouldn't be the one to blame.

Dane patted the seat and motioned for her to sit down.

"Forget it. Just tell me what's going on. Now." Aura crossed her arms over her chest. She knew she was being childish, but he couldn't lessen this blow…not by patting some seat…not with his soft, apologetic gaze.

The other officer cleared his throat anxiously, urging Dane to speak.

He exhaled long and hard, but she wouldn't back down.

"Say it." She dropped her hands to the edge of the table and leaned into him.

He stared up at her. "They've found another body in the lake. They found a credit card on the body. They think it may be Natalie."

Chapter Sixteen

Dane had given more than his fair share of bad news to families throughout the years and it always hurt to see the look of anguish and pain caused by words he was forced to speak. Yet telling Aura about Natalie's body was the hardest thing he'd ever had to do. From the look in her eyes it was clear it wasn't just Natalie who had been murdered...a part of Aura had died as well.

The drive to the scene was done in silence. There was nothing he could say or do to make this easier for her. There was no way he could soften the blow of losing her sister. So he simply held her hand. He couldn't help thinking that he was lucky that she was even letting him do this one simple thing after he had let her down. He'd failed. He'd failed to help her sister and to keep his promise.

This was his fault.

The body was already in the coroner's van when they arrived at the shoreline. From what the officer had told him, a man had been out on the lake fishing when he'd seen a body floating about a hundred yards from the beach. He'd pulled the woman from the water, hoping to revive her, but it had been too late.

"You ready?" Dane lifted Aura's hand and lightly kissed the back of her fingers.

Her eyes were glazed over and she nodded numbly like she wasn't there, instead trapped in her own mind. Guilt raged within him. He could never make up for his failings.

He walked around the patrol car and opened the door for her. If he did everything right for the rest of his life, he would never make up for the hurt that she was feeling. No matter how much love he showed her, no matter how much he tried to make up for the mistake he had made, he could never fill the hole in her heart that he'd created.

Aura's gaze stayed on the door, never rising to his face, as she stepped out of the car. His heart reeled like a car hit by a speeding bus.

"Aura?"

"Hmm?"

"I'm so sorry…" His voice trembled.

She put her hand on his shoulder, but said nothing. The snow crunched under her feet as she walked away.

He slammed the car door shut and moved after her. Parked by the coroner's van was the sergeant's patrol car. He was standing by the open door talking on his cell phone. Sarge's lips were pulled into a tight pucker; if they would have been his ass he would have been making diamonds.

When he saw Dane looking he beckoned him over. From the look on his face there was no question in Dane's mind—he was in trouble. He dragged his feet as he slowly turned. He could only guess who the sergeant was talking to who could force that specific facial contortion.

He glanced over to Aura who was standing on the edge of the icy water, staring in the direction of the fisherman's boat. The silver chrome bar that ran along the edge of the craft was smeared with blood. Aura couldn't be alone.

He spun toward Aura. Sarge could wait.

"Dane, get your ass over here!"

It was worse than he'd thought. In all his years on the force he couldn't remember a time when the sergeant had ever yelled at him. He begrudgingly made his way to the waiting pit bull.

"What's going on?" He mentally kicked himself for not staying silent. If he was going to get an ass-chewing he might as well make it quick and get it over with.

"I thought you had this." He pointed at the water. "And here I am finding another victim."

"You think it's the same person killing all these women?"

The sergeant's face darkened from tomato red to about-to-stroke burgundy. "Don't you think you should be the one telling me? I'm not the fucking investigating officer."

"Hey, I only just learned about this woman. Don't jump down my throat. I was off duty."

"If you had been doing your goddamned job instead of frolicking through the woods, getting a man hurt, and costing taxpayers' money, we wouldn't have this *fucking call.* Maybe you could have been catching a goddamned murderer."

"I was working on it." There was a steely edge to his voice, but he stopped—this was his boss. He couldn't go running into the dogfight baring his teeth. He needed to back out. He hadn't caused this mess, he was only trying to mop it up. "I'm sorry, Sarge. But we did find evidence. You know how it is—"

The man's color lightened to overly ripe tomato as he shut Dane up with a wave of his hand. "Look. I was just talking with the editor of the *Daily Interlake.* They're running a story about the last two victims and just caught wind of this…bullshit." He gestured to the boat. "I told you that you needed to get a handle on your investigation. I didn't tell you to go to the bar and hang out with our suspect."

"She's not a suspect. And I wasn't there with her. I mean I was, but not like that. We were there following a lead."

"What?" The sergeant leaned in and took a sniff. "You stink like the goddamned bar."

"Look, Sarge. I'm telling you we weren't there just socializing. We have reason to believe that a man named Shawn Gunner is possibly behind the murders. We have a video of him accosting Aura's sister, Natalie."

The sergeant stuffed his phone into the pocket of his thick winter coat. "Have you told Officer Grant about the development?"

"Why would I tell him? This is my investigation."

"Not anymore." He slammed the car door shut. "I think you've lost your objectivity. I don't think you're using your best *judgment* right now."

He bristled. "That's not true. I'm doing the best I can fucking do. I only just got the goddamned report from the crime lab. What the hell am I supposed to do with a purple cell phone, a knife, and two dead girls?"

"I understand you're frustrated." Some of the air seemed to leave the sergeant. "I'm not saying you're a bad cop. I'm just saying this may not be the best case for you to be assigned to. Between your brother, your ex-wife, and now this new woman…Well, I think you need to find a little distance. I'm reassigning the case to Grant."

"No!" He clenched his fists, but held back the urge to attack. "You can't do that to me."

"I can and I will. You need a break."

"No. Just give me a couple more days. I will get this." He couldn't let Aura down any more than he already had. The only chance he had of making up to her was by finding the killer. He needed this. "Please," he pleaded.

"Why in the hell should I keep you on this case? You've accomplished nothing and let another girl fall victim."

The sergeant was right, but he couldn't just walk away. "I'm telling you I *can do this*. Two more days. Please."

Officer Grant sauntered up behind him and threw his arm over Dane's shoulder like they were old football buddies. Dane shrugged the cocky little shit's arm off and silently hated himself for resorting to begging.

"Grant, I want to put you on hold on a little longer. Dane's going to be heading this case for a few more days."

"That's bullshit," Grant said in a rumble.

"Just listen to the words that are coming out of my mouth." Sarge pointed at his lips. "*Dane is leading the investigation.*"

Grant spun around and stomped off muttering profanities into the dusk.

"Thanks, Sarge." Dane felt small, like an overly disciplined child. He'd fucked up, but he wouldn't again.

"Don't give me any reason to regret this. If you do, you will be cleaning out the back of every patrol car from here to Gallatin County."

"I got it."

"You better."

Dane rushed toward Aura, the lake, and the boat that bobbed like the hand she'd found only a few days before. He could only hope that she hadn't seen her sister's body. That was one image she would never forget. He should know.

Aura had her arms wrapped around her as she sought comfort from the only person she could trust—herself. Her cheeks were pink and her warm breath made swirling white clouds in the cold evening air.

"You okay?" As soon as the words trickled from his lips he felt like an idiot. Of course she wasn't okay. She was standing at the edge of a crime scene that focused on retrieving and examining her sister's body. "I'm sorry…"

She looked down at the snowy ground. "Let's just not talk, okay?" Her voice was hoarse and ravaged by pain, and the sound ripped his heart from his chest.

He wanted to reach out and take her into his arms and make everything okay, but no matter what he did he couldn't make things right. This was one thing he couldn't fix or make any easier. She needed to mourn. To be angry. To hate him. But he would never hate her, only himself.

The overweight, wiry-haired coroner stood by the back door of the van with Officer Grant who was writing something down on his clipboard. Dane stepped over the yellow tape that protected the scene and made his way to the van. "Hey, Bill. Grant."

The man looked up from his paperwork and smiled like this was just another dead body, another day on the job. "Hey, Dane."

Dane held back the urge to cram the pudgy little man's smile down his throat. He stuffed his fists in the pocket of his jacket just as an extra measure. "Grant, what do you have on the vic?"

"Of course you come to *me* for answers, but do I head the investigation? *No...*" Grant snarled under his breath.

"Grant, just answer my goddamned questions. What do you know about the woman?"

"Well, the fisherman was out and saw her bobbing in the lake. Picked her up. Said he found a credit card with the name Natalie..." He glanced down at the paper. "Montgarten. No other form of ID."

"They find anything else on her? Jewelry? Cash?"

He flipped through the paper. "Nope. Just the card."

Who would just carry a credit card and no photo ID? Something about it struck him as odd. "Did you run an ID check on her?"

Grant looked up from his papers. "What do you think I am, some kind of idiot?"

Dane sniggered. The cocky little shit didn't want the real answer. "Did you find anything?"

"Well, it was pretty hard to ID the vic to the picture that came up. She kinda looks like the woman in the picture, but I'm not real sure."

"What? Why?" Dane grabbed the fabric of his coat pockets.

"Well..." Grant began.

Bill, the coroner, interrupted. "You wanna take a look?" The way he seemed to shift and jiggle reminded Dane of a neurotic, excitable little poodle.

He'd seen Natalie's picture, and he had to be of more use than the baby-faced Grant. "Let's see her." He pointed to the back of the van.

"Hope you haven't just eaten." The pudgy poodle chuckled as he pulled open the back door of the van and clambered up inside. "She has a good gunshot wound to the chest and one to the abdomen."

Dane cringed. What the hell was the man talking about? There was no such thing as a "good" gunshot wound. There was bad and really bad. No in-between. Every second he spent with this morbid little dog made him want to go and take a shower.

Bill wiggled excitedly as he slowly unzipped the bag one tooth at a time, like he took some kind of sick pleasure in the macabre scene within the body bag. The putrid scent of death was barely masked by the earthy, fishy aroma of the lake. Dane pulled his hand from his pocket and pushed his sleeve under his nose. No matter how many deaths he was around that was one scent he had a hard time getting over.

"You alright there, buddy?" Bill asked him with a stupid are-you-serious smile.

"Peachy. Hurry up."

Bill chuckled and flipped the bag open. The woman on the table was just as he had expected—brunette, early thirties, and clear evidence of several gunshot wounds. Was this the woman who'd owned the camisole that Aura had found in the truck?

Dane stared at the victim's face. Her eyes were closed, almost as if she were sleeping except that her face was a ghostly white. A little bit of red lipstick was still left on her bloodless lips, making them look even more sickening. She looked different from her picture. They would need to get fingerprints and, when Aura was ready, have her identify the woman.

He tried to swallow away the lump that rose in his throat.

Dane pulled the bag open a little bit further exposing her white sweater. Right where her heart would have sat was a gaping hole. Whoever had shot her had done so with a large caliber rifle or handgun. Maybe the crime lab would be able to identify the round and he could finally get some solid evidence.

When he pushed back the ragged edges of the cloth from the wound he noticed something strange—the edge of the skin was pink, not raw or as ragged as the cloth above it. Some of the woman's skin puckered and had a slight shininess to it, indicative of healing. He gasped as he dropped the cloth from his fingers.

"Aura!" He turned around and jumped out of the van leaving Bill to clean up the body. He'd love every goddamn second of it.

He rushed at her as she stood waiting behind the yellow tape. A little more aggressively than he'd intended, he grabbed her by the arm and pulled her toward the patrol car. "You and I need to talk…Now."

There was a resistance to her body and she pulled slightly as if she feared leaving the scene—or was it the fear of telling him the truth? Well, she couldn't hide it anymore. There was something going on, something strange, and he had a feeling she held the answers.

She looked like a trapped animal the way her eyes darted around, like she was looking for some type of escape. He opened the door to the car and motioned for her to sit down.

"You're going to sit here and talk to me. You aren't telling the whole truth and I know it. My job is on the line. Your sister is dead. If you want me to find out who did this, you need to tell me the truth. No more games."

Without argument, she sank down into the seat and put her hands over her face. Her shoulders trembled with silent sobs and he instantly hated himself for being so rough. "I'm sorry, Aura."

He shut her door and walked around to his side of the car, hating himself every step of the way. Everything was going downhill—he was breaking hearts, responsible for dead women, and close to losing his job, his credibility, and the only chance he'd had at a real relationship. It was all too much.

He got in and closed the door and then turned to Aura.

There was a heavy silence between them. The trembling of her shoulders lessened and she wiped away the tears from her cheeks and dabbed gently at her pink nose. "Was it really Natalie?"

"I think so…"

"Did she have a horse tattoo on her neck?" she asked, almost as if she begged for him to be lying.

He thought back to the red lipstick on her pale lips, her closed eyes, and her gaping chest wound. Though he tried, he couldn't recall seeing any tattoo. "Where was it?"

Aura brushed her fingers across the base of her neck. "About here. It's just a small black tattoo. She's had it for years."

There had been no tattoo, but he could have just missed it. He hadn't spent too much time inspecting the icy body.

He reached over and picked up her hand. "May I?" He started to push up the edge of her jacket.

Aura drew back slightly, but then nodded. Where there had first been the bloody teeth marks from the wolf's attack there was now nothing. No pink lines, no puckered scar and no evidence that she had never been attacked. He grabbed her other sleeve and pushed it back—there was nothing. Was he losing his mind?

He dropped her arm and stared at her. He had to have been going crazy. There was no possible way that she could have completely healed from the attack already. And there was no possible way that the victim could have even begun to heal from a chest wound over the heart. She would have been instantly killed.

The air in the car had turned cold and their breaths had started to fog the window, turning the world around them into a fading cloud of impossibilities.

Aura stared at him and after a minute finally moved to speak. "I…" She stopped as if she needed to regain her composure. "You're not going mad."

"That's funny. That's not how I'm feeling."

"There's a reasonable explanation for my arm."

"Really? Some miracle cream?" He scoffed.

She reached over, but he just stared at the palm of her hand.

"I have a special ability." She dropped her hand to the middle console, just close enough that he could feel her radiating warmth. Her body moved toward him, and he could smell the cold lake air on her skin. "So does…did…Natalie."

"Let me guess…You're a witch," he half joked.

She raised her eyebrows then gazed out the foggy windshield. "Well—"

He gasped. "You *have* to be kidding me."

"We aren't witches—though we have friends who are." She glanced back at him and there was a strange look of fear in her eyes.

"You have friends who are witches?" He nodded. He could handle a couple of Wiccans. He'd seen stranger things on his time on the force.

"A couple. They tend to come and go."

"Come and go? What do you mean?"

She let out a long sigh, like she was about to reveal that she was really a serial killer. "Natalie and I have been alive for over five hundred years."

Laughter bubbled up from his center. "You…" he said between laughs. "You are *hilarious*. I've heard some crazy shit in my day, but immortal life!?"

Aura picked at her fingernails. "I'm serious, Dane."

He wiped the tears from the corners of his eyes. "No, really… What's going on?"

"I'm a nymph. So is Natalie. We can seduce men. We can shape-shift. And we can be killed, but we're *almost* immortal."

"You're full of shit." He leaned back from her until he rested against the car door. "That's...that's impossible."

"I can assure you it isn't."

He took a second to collect his scattered thoughts. "Okay. If you can seduce men, did you seduce me?"

Aura chewed at her bottom lip. "Remember that day on the ranch? When you pushed me to the ground?"

In a second he was back there, lying on top of her. Kissing those damp lips. He could still remember the way her blonde hair fell upon the frost-laced grass. He could almost taste her honey-sweet lips. He shifted in his seat and cleared his throat. "What about it?"

"Did you intend to kiss me when you were pointing your gun at me?"

"No. Did you know I was going to kiss you?"

She gave him a coy smile. "That wasn't the only thing I had in mind."

"So you were using me? You've used me this entire time? You thought you could seduce me and get me to do your bidding?"

"I made a mistake. I thought you were like every other guy out there."

"You mean you thought you could get away with manipulating me?" He opened the car door and stepped out. He poked his head back in the car. "You don't know me. But I give a shit about people. I like to help people. You didn't need to fuck with me. I would have helped you find your sister. All you had to do was be honest." He slammed the door just as she started to talk.

He didn't want to hear her excuses. If they were anything like "We're nymphs" he was better off without her and her ridiculous lies.

The car door opened behind him and her footsteps rushed toward him. "Stop, Dane. You have to listen. I'm telling you the truth."

Dane spun around. "It's too much. You can't possibly expect me to believe that you are anything more than human. There are a lot of crazy things in the world, but a nymph isn't something I can just buy into. You'll just have to go find another man to *seduce*."

Reaching up, she grabbed him by his arms and shook him. "Stop. I know you don't get it. I don't expect you to. But you need to know Natalie wasn't human. Whoever killed her had to know this. They had to know what she was if they had any chance of bringing her down."

"Yeah, it was called a gun. They shot her, Aura. They shot her." His voice carried an unintentionally cold edge. "She wasn't immortal," he said, trying to be softer.

"Then it's not her. She would have healed." She pulled her arm out of her coat sleeve and exposed her perfect flesh to the biting wind. "Just like I did."

"I admit I don't understand *that*." He pulled out of her hands and pointed at her arm. The image of the woman's pink chest filtered into his mind. "And I don't understand what happened with the woman, but there was some amount of healing."

She coughed lightly as if trying to speak some words that choked her as they tried to come out. "Where was the gunshot?"

"Over her heart."

"There's no way that could have healed, unless she was more than human. And you know it."

He did know it. It didn't make sense. But he also knew she couldn't possibly be telling him the truth. Supernatural beings only existed in books.

Officer Grant sauntered over with his little black flashlight pointed at them. "You guys done having your little lover's quarrel?"

"Fuck off, Grant," Dane snarled.

"No, little Danish. You fuck off. I don't give a shit about whatever is going on between you and *her*." He pointed at Aura like she was a piece of garbage that had blown onto the beach.

"Listen here, you little prick, I know you think you're top shit, but let me tell you…you will treat my friend here with respect or I will take your pepper spray and stick it up your—"

Aura grabbed his arm. "Watch," she whispered.

She moved to Officer Grant and touched him softly upon the chest. "Don't get upset, Officer." Her voice was so sticky sweet it made his teeth hurt.

Aura couldn't think she really had some crazy ability. Grant had just treated her like trash. There was no way that he was going to fall for her luring charms.

"Aura?"

She shot him a look and he shut his mouth. This was her game and he could only stand by, watch, and when it didn't work he could tell her "I told you so." At least she could no longer lie. This would settle the matter of her thinking she was supernatural— though when the investigation was over, he would need to find her some help. There were meds for her kind of thinking.

Aura reached up and ran her fingers over the little bit of exposed skin on Grant's neck. The kid looked shocked at her familiar touch for a moment, but she smiled up at him and something changed. His eyes seemed to glaze over and his face seemed to glisten in spite of the cold.

A strange surge of jealousy filled Dane. She was sick. She needed help. And yet, in spite of it all, he still cared for her. He tried to shake off the feeling as he watched her trace her fingers along Grant's jawline.

"That's enough." He touched her shoulder, but she didn't look back.

"Grant?" she crooned.

The boy nodded.

"Do you want to kiss me?"

The boy nodded again.

"Would you be willing to do anything for me?"

The boy gave another trance-like nod.

The muscles in Dane's shoulders and back started to twitch—he really was losing his mind. It was slipping one neuron at a time. Pretty soon they would have to wrap him up and send him to the State Hospital in Warm Springs. It all didn't make sense.

"Grant…I want you to take off all of your clothes and take a swim in the lake. Okay?"

Officer Grant reached down and unzipped his coat. Aura stepped back as the kid stripped down to his underwear. His almost naked body steamed in the freezing air.

He looked up at Aura with, what Dane assumed to be, a seductive grin. "You want these off too?" He snapped the waistband of his form-fitted boxer briefs.

Things had gone far enough. "Aura, whatever you're doing you need to stop it right now."

She gave him a devilish smile. "Do you believe me?"

"Just because you can make a man strip down to his skivvies doesn't mean you are what you say you are."

"Oh really?" She turned back to Grant. "Swim."

The kid charged off into the night like he was some kind of Olympic gold medalist.

"Stop!" Dane called after him, but the kid didn't even slow down.

Everyone standing around the investigation turned and watched as Grant dove into the frigid water.

Dane rushed after him. "Somebody get him a blanket!"

Chapter Seventeen

The blanket covered Officer Grant from his pale, fur-covered knees to just under his protruding tiny pink nipples. A little part of Aura felt guilty as she stared at his blue-tinged lips. His skin was raw and red from the cold. It was unethical to use her power like she had, but she had been forced to prove her abilities to Dane.

When she looked over to him, Dane was still staring at her. His jaw was rigid and tense, almost as if instead of shock and excitement, he was angry. Maybe she should have lied and covered up the truth of her initial intentions, but he pleaded for honesty and she had complied. She should have known better. Few men wanted complete honesty—even when they asked for it.

"Get in the car and get warmed up," Dane ordered, as he pushed Grant into one of the waiting cars. "Aura. Come here."

She followed behind him as he led her to his patrol unit.

He spun around and leaned up against the car, like he needed it to hold him upright. "So you're telling me that you can do that to any man at any time?"

She nodded.

"How far can you take it? Can you get them to kill another person? To kill themselves?"

"Are you interrogating me?" she asked in a voice that dripped with danger.

He pushed his arms over his chest, as if protecting himself from the blows that she was thinking about landing. She'd told him a secret very few were privy to. Yet, he treated the knowledge with a trivial indifference and, more infuriating, contempt and suspicion.

She should have never opened up her heart, her mind, or her mouth. The desire to trust was best left to humans.

"I'm just asking, Aura. You have to understand that this is a new one for me. I just want to understand."

He was a cop. Of course he would want to put her in a little box. He needed her to be on the correct side of the line of right and wrong. There was no room in his life for a woman who kept secrets and didn't always make perfect choices. "I wouldn't kill anyone. Or have anyone killed. I'm not like that."

"What about your sister? Would she have been the kind to kill?"

Aura's mind moved to her sister. Had she been the type to kill? To let another kill for her?

When they had been young and wild, they'd moved from horse to woman and back without a thought. Life was safe, comfortable, and though not easy, it had been understandable. Most things were black and white. When humans had invaded their lives that safety disappeared. Trust quickly followed. Then their freedom. They could only run where they couldn't be captured.

"What are you thinking?" Dane asked, but it was almost an order. "Talk to me. Help me to understand."

Aura glanced around at the roaming police officers who were still going over the scene and talking to the fisherman.

"Just believe me. Neither of us is capable of killing." Their past had proven such a thing. Her eyes strayed to the black van where her sister's body lay. "I need to see her."

He moved to stand up, but then slumped back against the car. "I have more questions."

"I thought that you would. But please, before they take her away…I need to say goodbye."

Some of his hard edge seemed to crumble away as he looked at her. "Are you sure you want to see her?" He stood up and moved toward Aura, taking her hand in his. His hand was warm despite the bitter cold and she let his warmth soak into her as she stared at their joined hands. "Let them clean Natalie up first. Then I will take you to the crime lab and you can identify her."

There was no perfect time that she could think of that she would want to go and see her dead sister. "I need this, Dane. I need to see her. I need to see her to know that this is all real. That it isn't some strange, awful dream."

He got a strangled look on his face. "I understand that more than you know."

The way he said the words piqued her interest, but it could wait. "Let's go."

Dane pulled up the yellow tape and led her underneath. The pudgy curly-haired coroner gave her an out-of-place smile as he opened the back door to his van. "So you're her sister?"

Aura nodded and looked away from his upturned mouth.

"It's a real shame. I bet she was one hell of a looker."

There was an undertone of nastiness that made her skin crawl.

Dane moved protectively between her and the foul little man. "Bill, isn't there something else you should be doing?"

"Well, actually I was just about to call the lab and let them know I was about to be on my way to bring her in." Bill jingled his keys.

"Why don't you go do that somewhere else?" Dane pointed toward the wooden dock that bobbed a little further down the shoreline.

"You sure you got this?" Bill asked. "I mean, I can help if you need."

"No. That's fine. Go."

Aura was relieved as he walked away.

"I'm sorry about him," Dane said, squeezing her hand. "He's a bit *off*. I think it happens when someone is around death all the time. People tend to get a little strange."

She'd been called strange on a number of occasions, but she still couldn't empathize with the little penguin-shaped man that waddled down the beach. "Thanks for sending him away."

"You're welcome, but I sent him away for both of us. If he said one more stupid thing I was going to have to find some reason to arrest him." He turned to the van, stepped up, and lifted her hand, indicating for her to follow. "I know you said you were ready for this. To see Natalie, but I have to warn you, she's—"

"She is *dead*," Aura said. The words seemed to cement the wall that she had formed to protect herself from the reality that attacked from all fronts.

He squeezed her fingers as a miserable look centered on his face. "That's not what I was going to say."

"It doesn't change the fact that she's dead. She's not going to come back." Her voice cracked and she tried to swallow away the sadness that threatened to spill over. She had to keep control of herself. She needed to get through this, steel herself until she could get away from the prying eyes of the police that walked around the site.

Dane moved toward her like he wanted to take her into his arms, but she stepped back and dropped his hand. If she allowed him to comfort her, there would be no holding back. The sadness and anger that twisted just below the surface would break through and take her down and everyone around them. There would be no way she could open the bag that lay on the gurney in front of her and search for things that perhaps she could use to make sense of the tragedy. Perhaps she could find the answers, but only if she could stay in control of herself.

The bag was cold in her shaking fingers as she unzipped the little silver interlocking teeth. The scent of death wafted up from the bag, making a wave of nausea rise within her. The stench was unmistakable, decay, the deterioration of what was once vibrant and alive, but underneath the horrific scent was the fading scent of the woman—rich, earthy, mixed with the strange scent…of bird.

She jerked the zipper down past the woman's face and slung open the bag. A familiar face looked back up at her. Aura's heart pounded with excitement as she slapped her hands over her mouth. "Dane," she exclaimed from between her fingers. "It's not Natalie."

"What?" He stepped closer. "Are you sure?"

Did he really think that she didn't know her own sister?

"It's not her. It's Jenna Cygnini." She dropped her hands from her smiling lips. As hard as she tried, she couldn't make the smile lessen or her heart slow. She felt sorry for the woman she once knew, but was filled with overwhelming relief. Natalie could still be alive. She could still be waiting to be found. There was hope.

"Who is Jenna Cygnini?" He pulled out a pad of paper from his jacket and then stuffed it back in his pocket, as if he realized that she was going nowhere—that she wasn't just another person to be questioned. "Is she one of…" He glanced around, then leaned close. "You? You know a *nymph*?" He said the word in a barely audible whisper.

Relief that he believed her swept through her, making her feel the lightest she had since she'd arrived in Montana. There was no one around within hearing distance. "Yes. She's a swan-shifter from Idaho."

"What? She's a *what*?"

She reached down and rolled the woman slightly. The wet sweater gripped to the woman's flesh, but Aura forced the cloth down , exposing a patch of black ink at the base of her neck. "Look." She pointed at the black swan that was tattooed on her flesh. "It's their mark."

"Whose mark?"

"The swan-shifters. There are many groups of nymphs. Nat and I are part of the Mustang group."

He shook his head like he was trying to rattle the thought of what she was telling him around in his brain. "When you say *shifter* what exactly do you mean?"

She had forgotten. She hadn't told him about their other abilities. "I'm sorry. I don't want to freak you out."

"I'm way past freaked out. Just tell me what I need to know, okay?"

Should she tell him that she could never love? That if she gave her heart to a man that he was fated to die?

"I can't…" She couldn't say it. He was in no danger of loving her—not after she told him the entire truth. He hadn't seemed to want to take things that far, he cared and he was helpful, but it was all part of his job—except for the sex, but that had been her doing. She'd initiated their lovemaking. She'd seduced him.

Besides, once she told him the complete truth of who and what they are, he'd want no part of them. There were things that were forgivable, understandable, and acceptable to a man like Dane—but being a drifting, law-breaking, demi-god wasn't amongst those things. Love was an impossibility on all fronts.

Her fingers trembled on the edge of the bag. "I don't shift anymore."

"What does that mean? Why not?"

"A long time ago, Natalie and I use to be in our horse form most of the time. We were safe and could run free. When the settlers started moving into the Southwest, all of a sudden there were so many things to worry about. So many dangers."

"What happened to you?" There was an edge of sympathy in his gaze.

"To understand, you need to know that there are only a few ways that women of our kind can be killed."

"Wait. Now you're saying you can't be killed?"

"No, Dane. We can. That's the thing. It's simple if we are trapped. If someone pulls just a fistful of our hair, we die." She took a deep breath letting her thrashing heart slow.

"A long time ago, Natalie and I were running with the remnants of a once great herd when we were corralled. We were surrounded on all sides by the herd." For a moment all she could hear was the thundering of hooves and the fear-filled screams as the memory of the moment filled her thoughts. "I've never been more scared in my life. We had to shift back to our human form in order to escape before they culled the herd. We tried to save them, but before we could, it was too late. We saw every one of our friends, the wild horses, die."

She tried to hold back the tears, but chills rippled over her body. "They all died so some cows could have better grazing…It's all so wrong."

He stared at her in stunned silence for a moment and then dropped his gaze to the dead woman. "Do you think that Angela was killed by someone pulling her hair?"

Aura nodded.

"What about her hand?"

"I'm not sure how she lost it, but I think it was the reason she died. Everyone's body is covered with fine hairs. When we shift those fine hairs shift and become our fur. If she was in her horse form when she lost her hand, the loss would have been fatal. Too much hair was lost for her to survive."

Dane leaned his body against the gurney as if it could carry some of the burden of the shock from her revelation. "And your sister still shifts? I don't understand it."

"Natalie loves to shift. She's a beautiful brown bay. She's the most beautiful horse you've ever seen, strong in the shoulders, glistening mane, and perfect white socks on her feet—she was the horse in the video."

He blinked as he must have tried to make sense of her admission. Dane reached down and pushed her fingers from the bag. He reverently moved the sweater back over Jenna's arm, then zipped the bag closed. "So your sister is a horse. This lady is a swan. And you're a..."

"Mustang as well. It's been a long time since my last shift, but when I do, I'm a palomino. Natalie always used to say she was jealous of my canter, but I never believed her."

"Canter..." he mumbled, shaking his head. "Okay." He sighed as he must have resigned himself to the fact she had told the truth. "So you can seduce and shift. Can you do anything else? Can you do magic?"

"If you mean like a sorcerer or a witch—no. Sometimes we have a gift. Not every nymph has one, but I do."

"And what is this gift?"

She wanted to escape from the cage of his questions, but she couldn't. Somewhere along the way she had come to respect him and part of that respect was the ability to be honest—whether or not he would believe her or understand was another matter entirely. But she cared for him enough to be honest—to submit.

"I can talk to animals. In our world we call it empathic."

He stood silently, staring at her over the dead body of the swan-shifter. The corners of his lips quivered and then pulled into an awkward smile as laughter filled the mobile tin casket. "You're a seducing Doctor Doolittle!" His laughter echoed off the inside of the van and bounced out into the night like a child's lost ball. "That's amazing!"

It confused her that he would have a problem with her right up until the point that she could talk to animals, and then he thought it was amazing. Being an empathic was amazing, but it surprised her that this would be the ability that he would accept. Perhaps it was the animal psychics on late night television infomercials or the whack-jobs on the animal shows that proclaimed they could communicate with animals, but something about this ability must have been something he could finally understand. Something he could put inside the box. This was something he could grasp and cling to like a fumbling rock climber on the ledge of understanding when the reality around him had dramatically given way.

She smiled and took his hand and led him out of the van. His laughter and the lapping of the water upon the shore was the only noise. Everyone stared at him.

Aura turned to him. "If you want to stay on this investigation you better stop laughing." She pointed over at the sergeant's confused expression. "I think they're starting to wonder if you're losing it."

Dane clamped his lips shut, but his body still shook with unspent laughter. Trying to cover his laughter, he turned to the van and slammed the doors shut. He held his hands on the metal for a second until the shaking of his shoulders stopped.

The sergeant, who had been talking to the fisherman, sauntered over. "Dane, what's going on here?"

Dane turned and faced the firing squad. "We identified the victim. It's not Natalie Montgarten. The woman's name is Jenna Cygnini. She's a woman out of Idaho."

The sergeant frowned. "And how do you know this?"

Aura stepped up for her turn. "I know her. She's a friend of a friend."

The only reaction the sergeant gave her was a terse raise of his eyebrow. He turned to Dane. "Find out who did this." He reached in his jacket and pulled out a piece of paper. "Here's the credit card number. I'm running a check on it. You will find the paperwork in your file when you get to work in the morning."

Dane took the slip of paper and slid it into his pocket. "Got it."

"Now I want you and Aura to go home. Get some rest. And think about how you're going to solve this case." The sergeant turned back to the fisherman. He looked back at them over his shoulder. "Remember. Two days." He put up two fingers, like a pair of scissors that waited to snip away Dane's reputation.

Chapter Eighteen

"You're still staying here?" Dane looked at the campground sign.

"It's fine, really. I like staying in my trailer." Aura looked up at him with her tired eyes and he felt instantly guilty.

He didn't know her financial situation, maybe she couldn't afford to stay at a hotel. Or maybe she'd just planned on passing through, didn't want to set down roots, or was it a nymph thing?

Dane slowed down the car, and looked down the dirt road that led to the main camping area. "It's too cold to be staying outside. The news is saying it's supposed to get close to zero tonight."

"I'm sleeping in the horse trailer's tack room. I'm used to it. Besides, we spent last night out in the same weather and we were fine, weren't we?"

Faint warmth moved through his cheeks as he thought about her lying in his arms, out in the moonlight with only the stars and the mountains watching. It was a night he would never forget. Suddenly he realized he'd made love to a nymph—a goddess. He couldn't hold back his smile. "Are you going to tell me you don't freeze because you're a nymph?"

She laughed tiredly. "I never really thought about it, but I guess we can't."

He started to turn the car into the drive, but instead merely pulled to the side of the road. "How about you come over to my place and you can take a shower and rest. That way I don't have to worry about you being alone."

She looked at him wryly. "What do you think you're going to do with me when you take me to your house?"

His smile widened. "I swear I only have the most honorable of intentions in mind." He instantly visualized her lying naked on his bed. "Just thought you could use a soft bed and a hot shower." His thoughts twisted to envisioning her standing in the glass walls of his shower, steam rising around her, fogging up the windows. He tried to ignore the way his pants grew tighter.

"Honorable, right." She laughed.

"I swear. I will not touch you..." He put his hand over his heart. "Even if you beg. You need your rest."

Her happy laughter rippled through the tension that had filled the car since they'd left the crime scene. The sound made relief swell inside his chest. It felt good to hear her really laugh again.

Checking over his shoulder, he eased the car back onto the highway and drove toward his house. An odd sense of excitement mixed with his sense of relief. He could protect her from anyone and maybe get a chance to really understand her. There were so many questions he had about her and her kind.

While he drove, she told him a short history of her kind from Epione to modern day. His mind felt as if it was floating with the new wealth of knowledge. The new reality that she was presenting was like a dream that he couldn't fully grasp. He couldn't help feeling like he'd finally broken into sitting at the cool kids table— that he was part of some elite class of beings that knew the truth.

"Jenna had some problems with who and what she was," Aura continued as she reached over and took his hand. "Sometimes it happens. They can't handle the nature of the beast."

"What do you mean *the nature of the beast*?" He looked over at Aura.

She caught his eyes, but guiltily glanced away.

"I'd like to think we are past you lying to me. Don't you know you can tell me the truth about anything? You don't see me running away, do you?" He threaded his fingers between hers and pulled her hand over his heart. "I want to help you the best that I can. I care about you."

"That's what I'm afraid of," she said half under her breath.

He pulled the car into the driveway and parked. "What do you mean by that? Don't you want me to care about you? I know it took a lot to tell me the truth. I don't really get it yet, but I will with time."

She hesitated for a moment, as if she were weighing her options. "I care about you too." He heard the words, but the tone was that of a break-up. "But you and I, we can't be together. We're too different."

He wanted to tell her she was wrong, that they could make a relationship work, that all they needed was a little time and they could work out their problems. But all he could think of was Angela. They had been different as well, she had been similar to Aura in the fact that she'd been a drifter, and look at where they had ended up.

Maybe it wasn't such a bad thing to avoid having a relationship. What they had *worked*. At least that's what he forced himself to think. In his heart, he could feel the sharp edge of the lie cutting away at his resolve.

"I get it." He got out of the door and went around and helped her out of the car, giving himself a moment to think.

She kept looking at him, like she was waiting for him to argue with her or for him to get upset, but he just walked silently to the front door and opened up the lock. If she didn't want a relationship, he didn't either. She was the one running this thing between them, he couldn't force anything.

"Do you want to take a shower first?" he asked, pointing down the narrow hallway to the guest bath. "I think I have a set of clothes around here that might fit you."

She wrapped her arms around her body and stared down the hall. "Yeah, that would be great."

He tried to ignore the awkward silence between them and he tried to think of something to say, but there was nothing. If he brought up Natalie she'd go off and they'd probably end up running around the woods all night tracking down leads, but they both needed their rest. His head hurt and the muscles were still stiff and sore from the horseback ride the day before.

Dane made his way to his room as Aura followed. She kept her arms around her as if she was afraid to touch anything in his life and leave her mark. What was she so afraid of?

As Aura took her shower Dane changed the sheets on his bed and set up the couch for himself. She could have the bed. She needed a little bit of comfort—and who knew, maybe she'd wake up and decide that there was something that they needed to explore between them. Maybe she would come to understand how much he cared about her, how much he wanted her in his life.

But for her to know…he had to say something.

She came out of the bathroom still toweling her hair dry. At the end of the hall there was a bookcase filled with dust-covered pictures and stacks of well-read books. Not noticing him standing there and watching, Aura walked to the end of the hallway and looked over the contents. He walked to her, letting her have a moment to peer into his life and memories.

He stopped next to her. "Good shower?"

"Oh hey," she said, dropping her towel over her arm. "Yeah, the shower was great, thanks. Nice and relaxing."

He tried to ignore the reawakened images of her in his shower as he cleared his throat.

There on the top shelf, just at eye level, was the only award he'd ever won and he blushed slightly as Aura picked up the little wood and brass plaque.

"Lifesaving Medal awarded to Flathead County Deputy Dane Burke. In grateful appreciation of your outstanding police performance, in saving of a human life and the display of compassion, initiative, capability, and attention to duty, thereby earning respect and admiration for himself and the Department." A wide smile spread across her face. "You must be really proud."

"It wasn't like that. Anyone on the force would have done what I did. I just happened to be at the right place at the right time."

"What happened?" She ran her fingers lovingly over the edge of the frame.

That cold day three years ago had seemed much like today—he'd been standing on the edge of the lakeside after helping load a dead woman into a body bag.

"It was a few years back. A family had come up to Montana for a family trip and thought they could go out on the lake in a rickety old boat." He pointed at a picture he'd taken of Flathead Lake. "That place is one of the largest freshwater lakes in the U.S. and one of the coldest. It's fed in the summertime by snow runoff. It gets real deep in places. In the winter the lake has only been known to completely freeze over once and the ice didn't last long."

He lifted the plaque from her hands and sat it back on the bookshelf, wiping some of the dust off in a feeble attempt to cover his lack of housekeeping skills. "Of course they got stuck out there and the wind picked up. We don't know what really happened from there, the little girl was only three. But it sounded like the father had tried to row with his arms, but got tossed overboard. The mom jumped in to save him, not knowing how cold the water was…or how quickly hypothermia can set in."

He watched her shiver beneath his oversized tee.

"We got to the little girl just in time. The boat had begun to take on water and she developed hypothermia from the exposure. I had to hold her until the medics showed up. They said I saved her life, but I'm telling you it was exactly what anyone else would have done. She was just a little frightened girl."

He'd been plagued with thoughts of that day for months afterward, until he'd finally gotten up the balls to go and see the psychologist. Even now, once in a while, he would have the reoccurring nightmares. They would take turns with the night at the barn. Each nightmare was horrific and terrifying in its own cruel way.

"Is the little girl okay?" Aura asked.

"Yeah, I see her from time to time. She moved in with her grandparents who don't live too far from here. They seem to take really great care of her."

Aura looked back at the plaque. "I don't know how you do it all. I don't think I could deal with all the horrible things you have to deal with. It has to be a lot."

Dane lifted the towel from Aura's arm and wiped away a droplet of water that fell from her hair and had started to twist down her forehead. She moved closer, like she wanted to take him in her arms like he had done with the little girl, but she stopped short and turned back to the shelf.

An unexpected sadness formed in his heart. He couldn't kiss her full sweet lips and tell her it would all be okay. She couldn't open her arms and let him find solace in her embrace. They were just like that little boat sitting out in the cold water, bobbing away, simply waiting and hoping that they would make it through the day. But there was no rescue coming for him or for her—unless it came from the other.

"Who are all of these people?" she asked, pointing to a picture of him and his family as they stood outside of the bright red barn at the Diamond.

"Oh, that's my mom and dad." He pointed to the familiar pair at the far left of the picture. "That's Zeb next to them, then me."

"You guys look really happy. How old were you here? Sixteen?"

He wrestled the thoughts of the little girl from his mind, but unfortunately she was quickly replaced with thoughts of his mother. "Yeah, I guess I was about that. This photo was taken a year before…"

"Before what?"

"Before I found my mother in the barn…she…she'd had an accident." The words filled his mouth with acid. The smell of the ash was still fresh in his mind though it had been years before.

"Do you mind me asking what happened?"

He'd lectured her on honesty in the car and as badly as he didn't want to tell her about his past, he knew it couldn't be avoided without him looking like a hypocrite. She had opened up to him, telling him about who she was, when she could have kept up her front. It was time to let her in, at least enough for her to know that he trusted her as much as any cop could trust another person.

"My mother was a smoker. She knew better than going in the barn to light up, but she was trying to hide it from my dad. Of course, he knew but he always pretended to not notice the way her clothes smelled of cigarette smoke."

"It was a senseless accident, and I tried to save her, but the burns were too severe." The thought of his mother made his heart clench and tears well in his eyes. "My father died not long after from a heart attack. And when I left the ranch, I guess I thought I left it all behind. But I've been wrong. I think I've just been running. Trying to save the ones I can."

"I'm so sorry, Dane. I shouldn't have asked."

"Yeah, well, I guess shit happens to everybody. My brother tore down what was left of the burned out barn after I left."

"So your dad left the place to Zeb?" Her cheeks flamed, as if she instantly felt shame for continuing to pry into his past, but he didn't mind.

"No." He cleared his throat. "He left it to both of us, but after I left, Zeb took over the running of the place. After the accident and everything that had gone on at that place…well I just didn't want to be there anymore. There were too many memories. Plus, I hate to admit it, but I really hate working with cows." His laughter echoed through the dusty house.

"What about horses?" She gave him a seductive smile.

Dane moved into her and wrapped his arms around her and could feel her moist skin beneath his old tee-shirt. "I'm always up for a good ride," he whispered, pulling her sweet, freshly washed scent deep into his lungs.

She looked up at him and there was a light in her eyes that he recognized from the night they'd spent on the mountain. She wanted this...even if she had said she didn't. He leaned down and feathered his lips against hers. He didn't want to take this fast. If this was his last chance to make love to this beautiful goddess he was going to relish every second of it—even if he had to think about football to make himself go a little further.

She took his lip in her teeth and nipped, the pain only made him want her more. He tightened his arms around her and pulled her against him, showing her exactly how much he needed to feel her again.

Aura ran her hands up his chest and ran her thumb over the cloth above his nipple, making it harden like the rest of him. Dane ran his hands down to the bottom of her shirt and lifted up the edge, he slid his fingers underneath and felt her buttery smooth skin. He found the line of her panties across her ass. Finding the top of the silk, he pushed his fingers under the thin fabric.

Her palms moved over his chest and she pushed gently as she released his lip from her sucking mouth.

"Dane," she said, between heavy breaths. "We can't do this. Not now."

• • •

The clock ticked away, marking each second that passed while Aura imagined him lying out on the couch. Was he thinking of her? Was he thinking of the things that could have just happened between then? Or what had happened in the past?

Her hands slipped down under her panties as she thought about the feel of him inside of her. She had wanted him again, there was no question, but there was so much at stake—and most fragile was their hearts. He couldn't love her and more importantly, she couldn't love him. She couldn't risk feeling his body against hers, the heat of his breath on her skin, or the way he made her heart flutter to life.

The moisture under her fingers grew as she envisioned his body between her legs, him thrusting inside of her like there would be no end to their lovemaking. She fantasized tiptoeing out into the living room and finding him in the night—hungry for her touch. With her other hand, she reached up and ran her finger over her lips, trying to mimic his kiss. Her fingers felt cold, familiar, and unwelcome—and they left her wanting.

Could she risk going to him?

Aura closed her eyes. The motion of her fingers and the lulling warmth filled her body, relaxing her mind and making her body her only focus. She was growing closer by the second to finding a fleeting moment of bliss.

Her breath came in cutting jags as the sound of a knock on the door broke her body-centered trance.

"Aura," Dane whispered, "are you still awake?"

She silently tried to catch her breath and slow her heart from pounding out of her chest. She didn't know what to do. If she stayed silent, he would probably never come back to her. What they had together would be gone. The morning would come and they would treat each other as strangers. If she answered, he would know that she had been lying here thinking of him. If he opened the door he would see her sweating face and know what she had been doing—and in her heart she knew he would find his way into her bed.

There was a squeak as he turned away from the door and his footfalls moved down the hall and away from her.

Throwing back the sheets, she mentally threw back her defenses. She loved him. Even if she tried to deny it, she wanted him. Not just now, but for the rest of her life. He was already in danger—and had been from the moment he'd stepped foot into her life.

She ran to the door, flipped on the lights, and threw the door open. "Dane!" she cried.

He turned around slowly, as if he knew what would come of his facing her. But he didn't know.

"I can't love you. You mustn't love me. My kind can't have love."

He stopped and gave her a look of dismissive disbelief. "Everyone can love." He stepped toward her and put his hand on her chest, right over her heart. "Everyone's heart beats. Yours beats. Mine beats….and when I'm around you there's something more. I—"

She pressed her finger over his lips. "You can't say it. If you say it, you will die."

His forehead collected into a mess of fine wrinkles as he shook his head.

"Yes," she said, pulling her finger from his lips. "All nymphs are cursed. If we fall in love, the man we fall in love with is cursed to die."

"I don't believe in curses."

"There have been thousands of men who dared to utter what you just said—and they all paid the ultimate price for their choice to not believe."

"Would it make you feel better if I tell you I believe in the curse? But what if I just don't give a damn?" Aura ran her hands up his back like she could wipe away his foolish thinking, but he wouldn't have it. "I don't care if my life is at risk. My life's always at risk—I'm a cop."

"Even if you don't care—I do. I love you." She tried to bury her face in his chest, but he reached down and took her chin in his rough fingers. Before she could pull back he owned her lips with his, their teeth knocked together with his forceful passion.

Her thoughts fluttered to Lord Tennyson who once said 'It was better to have loved and lost, than never to have loved at all.' She had heard the quote often, but not until here and now had she truly believed the man. Now as she stared at the golden flecks in Dane's eyes she was at a loss for logical thought. She needed to get lost, let herself be devoured by the sweet light in his eyes, the motion of his body, and the love in her heart.

His kiss softened and he drew back slightly, softly brushing his tongue over her bottom lip, tasting her like a summer-ripened peach. The flick of his tongue made her already moist center quiver with desire for the greatness he had to offer.

She tried to pull out of his arms to lead him to the soft bed, but he wouldn't allow her to move. Reading her body's desire, he moved her to the rough carpet, never letting his lips move away from hers. She opened her legs and let his body rest upon hers, but he had no intention of resting. Instead, he reached down with both hands and pushed up her shirt. His kiss deepened and he reached down to her panties. He pulled the fabric tight and ripped open the seam then repeated the action on the other side.

Aura lifted her hips, letting him slip the silken panties away from her wanting body. He broke away from their kiss for a moment and moved between her legs. His pants landed on the floor next to her, but she barely noticed. Dane pressed his hot, naked flesh against her, taking his time as he gently rubbed himself against her wetness. She moaned and threw back her head in carnal desire.

His body shook with wicked laughter as he rubbed harder, mimicking the motions that she'd been making with her fingers only minutes before. If he wasn't careful the fun would never begin. She let her body speak as she lifted her hips and tried to force him to enter her. He ground his body against her again and his body shook with excitement.

"Please…" she moaned.

He traced his lips over her neck and down her collarbone. He feathered his tongue down her chest in between kisses until he circled her nipple. She sucked in a heavy breath as he pulled her into his mouth. She tried to force her body to calm, to hold off from the release that threatened to spill over.

"Dane…" she begged.

His mouth released her hardened nipple and he moved as if to take the other, but stopped and drove inside of her, catching her by surprise. Her body bucked with unbridled excitement and euphoria. She'd never felt anything as good as him inside of her.

The rough carpet scratched at her skin, but she didn't care—the pain only made the pleasure that much sweeter. He slowed, taking his time as he kissed everywhere his mouth could reach without his leaving her. She had never been more satisfied.

Chapter Nineteen

His knees were covered in angry rug burns and his back ached from their hours of lovemaking, but the smile on Dane's face hadn't wavered all morning—that was until he walked into the station. There was a manila envelope perfectly centered in the middle of his desk with the sergeant standing in front, like a cautious sentinel.

Of course Aura had refused to be left behind, so she was forced to wait outside in the main lobby while he picked up his assignment and the dreaded envelope.

The sergeant nodded when he saw Dane walk into the room. "I thought you were never going to get here. Jesus, what did you do? Stop at the gas station for a doughnut?"

Dane looked down at his watch. "It's only six twenty, I'm ten minutes early. What are you talking about?"

"I've been waiting and so has Officer Grant." He pointed over at the stewing Grant, who kept glancing over from his chair as if he was just waiting for the sergeant to call him over.

Was that why Sarge had been waiting? So he could kick him off the case and let the little jackass take over? If that was it, why hadn't he just pulled him like he'd threatened at the lake? Or had he thought about what Dane had asked and reneged on his decision?

Well, he wasn't going to have it. He might be taken off the case, but he wasn't going to stop looking. The woman he loved depended on him. There would be no stopping them until he had Natalie in his possession.

"As far as I give a shit, Officer Grant can keep on waiting." He jerked his thumb toward the slobbering kid.

The sergeant chuckled. "Easy now." He grabbed the envelope off the desk and thrust it at Dane like it was filled with classified documents he'd stolen from the FBI. "You have to take a look at what we were able to dig up. Not only did we find out where the woman had been staying, but we also finally got an ID on the unidentified dead woman we found with Angela. Found out that she's some woman named Katarina Homeros. Comes from Crete. She's been involved in some risky business involving money laundering and bribery in the last year. Most recently she was picked up for animal cruelty. Nasty woman, that one."

"Did they run a test for Clomiphene on the newest vic—Jenna?" Dane grabbed the envelope and stuffed it under his arm. The information could wait until he was in the privacy of his patrol car and out from under the nose of the waiting vulture.

"Early tests seemed to confirm that it was present, but you know how they work…everything is tentative."

Tentative with the crime lab was good enough for him to assume that these women were all connected to the same murderer. They were close. They would find whoever was behind the crimes. He silently prayed to God that Natalie had nothing to do with the murders and was nothing more than a missing woman.

"Great." He turned to walk away.

"And Dane?"

He looked back over his shoulder. "Yes, sir?"

"Remember, after today you only have one more day." The sergeant put up his finger with the zest of a well-practiced proctologist prepping for an exam. "Get your shit together."

The door slammed shut behind Dane as he made his way out to the lobby. Aura looked up at him—her cheeks were still flush from their lovemaking and his smile returned. He held up the files. "We have a solid lead. They located the hotel where the card was last used."

"Really?" She stood up excitedly. "Let's go."

The icy air nipped at his skin as they got into the car. He ripped open the envelope like a kid opening a Christmas present. They finally had some kind of answers—something solid. Hopefully it would prove to be the answers they were looking for.

The stiff papers dropped into his lap and he looked down at the credit card company's list of transactions for the last year on Natalie's card. Everything seemed normal up until the last week. She'd gone from buying groceries, gas, and paying routine bills to going to bars, nightclubs, and pricey hotels.

The last charge had been to a Best Western in Kalispell, not far from the station and only a few miles from Somers. It sat right at the intersection of Highways 93 and 82—almost the perfect place for someone who wanted to make a fast getaway. If they were lucky they could get there and find the man the bartender had seen Jenna with the night they had gone there. Maybe if they hurried they could get to him before he had time to realize he'd thrown away his cash source along with his victim's body.

"The place isn't too far from here. I think we can get there in about ten minutes. Maybe we can see if we can find Shawn's truck." He thumbed through the file. Everything else after the credit card history was pretty straightforward, a workup on the other woman they'd finally identified. Her criminal record was all relatively new crimes and there was a copy of her Visa and her Greek passport with her small picture, but there was nothing to indicate why the murderer would have picked her to be a victim.

He thrust the papers toward Aura and started the car. "Take a look at these and see if you can see anything else that we are going to need to know."

The heater blew the papers around in her hand, but they were going nowhere from the look of her white knuckles. "You didn't tell me they identified the other woman," she said, breathlessly.

"Yes, she's some woman out of Greece or something."

"She's not just *some woman*…" She lifted the papers so he could look at them. "She's *Katarina Homeros.*"

He shrugged. "That means nothing to me. Should it?"

"She's a nymph. And not just any nymph. She used to be the leader of the Sisterhood of Epione."

He had no idea what she was talking about. As hard as he tried, he couldn't place the Sisterhood of Epione anywhere in his memory. "Okay. Do you think that has anything to do with her murder?"

"Don't you know what this means?"

"Every single woman who has been found murdered has been a nymph."

• • •

Aura tried to stay calm as she stared over at the bewildered Dane. Her stomach tensed until it felt like a giant knot of emotions. Whoever was behind all of these murders knew their secret—the fact that they could only die if their hair or skin was pulled or destroyed.

"Wait. Angela…Angela was a nymph?" Dane asked, trying to pull together the threads of evidence as he tried to understand the whole picture.

Aura nodded. "She was a horse-shifter like Natalie and I."

His bewildered expression turned to one of amazement and shock. "I never knew."

"Most nymphs never tell humans the truth. Most people wouldn't understand."

He nodded as if he could empathize with the rest of his kind. "Angela wasn't ever very forthcoming."

"I'm sorry, Dane."

"Were Angela and all these women part of this Sisterhood?"

"Every nymph is connected to the Sisterhood. They are like the ruling party of all nymphs. Crete, where Katarina was from, is like our holy Mecca. It's where our kind were first born and bred. It is all nymphs' home, even if we weren't born there."

She dropped the papers back down and stared at Katarina's picture. "And I guess you could say the Sisterhood is the nymph's equivalent of the Vatican. Though in the last century, since industrialization, they haven't played as strong of a role in our governing. Most nymphs are well aware of the implications of who, and what we are, and what is expected of us. Not that we are always perfect, but they assume that our local governments are capable of keeping us in check. When that doesn't happen then they'll intercede, but it has always been rare."

She thought about Crete and the secrets that were now likely to be exposed. "I don't know how the Sisterhood is going to handle this, but they don't like to have dead nymphs lying around. This would be the first incident of its kind in a long time—if ever."

She thought back to last year's event with Beau Morris and Ariadne Papadakis in Crete. Ariadne had changed the fate of many nymphs. No longer were they under the thumb of Katarina Homeros—the lying, deceitful breaker of the magical staff of Epione.

Dane stared at her as he must have tried to comprehend everything she had told him. "So this Katarina was like the Pope until recently?"

"Exactly. Last year, she was not overthrown exactly, but she was removed from power by another nymph from Crete—Ariadne, I think. She didn't like the way the group was being run, she wasn't alone, but she ended up digging up some secrets from Katarina's past that put the whole order of our way of life in question. Many of our kind were upset when the truth came out about how Epione's healing staff had been broken."

"Do you think there are some nymphs who are still holding a grudge?"

Aura thought for a moment. There were hundreds, if not thousands, of nymphs around the world, but she'd never met one that seemed hell-bent on killing Katarina or any other nymph—but that was as far as she knew. Nymphs were, in some aspects, no different than humans—anger, jealousy, and rage were just as alive and well in their community as they were in human civilization. It was hard to assume that there wouldn't be someone somewhere that wanted to get back at Katarina for her lies—but it was hard to believe that Natalie was one of them. She wasn't the type to hold a grudge. Especially a grudge against a woman that she knew only through the nymph world, but had never met in person.

"Maybe, but I don't know what that would have to do with the other nymphs that have been killed. Did Angela have anything to do with the Sisterhood?"

From the look on Dane's face she knew instantly that she had made a mistake.

"Look, I hadn't even really known what a nymph was until you told me what you were. Angela never told me anything about her other life. She didn't love me, remember?"

Her heart wrenched in her chest. She hadn't meant to rub salt into his wounds. "I'm sorry, Dane. But if it helps you, she must have cared about you enough to try and not love you—she didn't want to see you get hurt. She didn't want you to get killed because of the curse."

"Are you really trying to tell me that she didn't love me because she cared about me? That doesn't make any goddamned sense." He slammed his opened hand against the steering wheel and then turned to her. "Look at you and me...You were willing to look past the curse because you care about me. You couldn't help but to love me. Right?"

The knot tightened in her stomach. She had been foolish to let her emotions cloud her judgment, but there was no going back now. She loved him and there was nothing either of them could do to change the way she felt.

"Angela must have been stronger than I am." Aura stared down at her fingers. "I love you, but that doesn't mean that I should have let myself feel this way. She was able to put herself in an emotional bubble—just what I should have done."

Dane reached over and made her put down the papers. "You don't regret falling in love with me, do you?" He took her hands and, pressing them together, pulled them to his lips. He kissed the edges of her fingers. "I don't regret falling in love with you. It's the only good decision I've ever made when it has come to my life."

"That is *if* you don't die." She gently pulled her fingers from his. "Maybe it's not such a bad idea to let Officer Grant take over the investigation. You and I can…"

"Go rogue?" Dane looked up at the station. "Is that what you want? To let someone else try and find Natalie?"

She knew what she was asking him. The man cared more for his work than anything else in his life. When she'd met him, there was no chance that he would have given up his professional edge for her or anyone else. Step by step, moment by moment, he'd been changing for her, going against his sergeant and putting himself on the line to find Natalie.

She could only repay him by protecting him. "If it means keeping you safe." As the words tumbled from her lips she knew there was no keeping him safe.

Even if she kept him in a bubble there was nothing that would stop Zeus from inflicting the curse's fate. It wasn't a matter of if the god would punish her for falling in love; it was only a matter of when. They may have a few days or they may have a few years, but regardless, it wouldn't be enough time and it would be hard to justify her actions if something was to happen to Dane.

They sat in silence. Dane looked over at her and opened his mouth. He stared at her, his lips trembling as he struggled to speak.

"Let's just go," she offered, in a weak attempt to make up for everything she had done to him. "Let's find Shawn. Maybe he can point us toward Natalie."

He reached over and ran his thumb over her cheek. "I love you. It doesn't matter to me if I die today, tomorrow, or in fifty years. I got the chance to love you and it's been the most amazing thing I've experienced in my life."

Aura reached up and took his hand. "I love you too. And I'm sorry—"

Before she could finish her sentence he rushed across the car and stole her lips. There was no gentleness, only the harsh passion of love and the reality of their plight. They were two sinking ships, but they would go down together.

Dane pulled back from her lips and gave her a look that had even more passion than their kiss. "If you want…If it's really what you want, I will go in there and tell Grant to take over the case."

The love in her heart grew, pushing the boundary of her heart's ability to fill with love. "Thank you. I know how much your job and this case means to you…" She paused. Should she tell him to quit the case? They could go out on their own, unencumbered by the weight of the badge that was pinned to his chest.

Aura stared at the badge. Lifting her hand, she trailed her fingertips over the cold metal. Even if Dane wasn't wearing the emblem it didn't change the man he was on the inside. They would follow the same path whether or not he was wearing it. He would never do something that he knew was wrong.

Except loving her …

"Let's find Shawn together. I'll protect you. Nothing will happen to you as long as I'm here." She trailed her fingers from his badge to his jacket's zipper and pulled it up. "I promise."

He smirked as he pulled down the zipper just enough to show his uniform's collar. "They probably won't even be there. It will be a long shot to find them."

Aura sat back in her seat. "A long shot is better than no shot at all."

Chapter Twenty

The hotel was surrounded by a large parking lot still filled with cars with skis strapped to their roofs and *Love to board* bumper stickers on several of the ski-less Subarus. A pair of blurry-eyed college age kids, wearing snow pants and carrying their coats, stumbled out of the front door of the hotel and made their way to their little green Forester.

From the looks of the square-cut beams and the finely laid stonework on the exterior of the building, the hotel was nice. It was the kind of place that Natalie would have loved to stay as it echoed the charm of the timbered mountains that surrounded the western-infused building. If Aura had to guess, in the center of the lobby there was probably a large river rock fireplace, above it hanging a bull elk mount that someone had picked up from a taxidermy shop.

Dane turned the corner to the back lot. Parked in the farthest corner was a silver GMC. As they approached she could make out the red, white, and blue Idaho license plate. But she would have recognized her sister's ex-husband's truck anywhere.

"There!" She pointed at the older model half-ton truck.

"Is that his? For sure?" Dane asked hesitantly, as if he couldn't believe they had actually found what they were looking for.

"Positive." She shifted in her seat excitedly. They were going to get Natalie. Aura could feel it. "What are we going to do? Do you want to go in?"

Dane reached down and talked into the walkie-talkie that was clipped to his chest. "Two-nine-seven, two-six-five we are on scene and going into the Best Western, Somers..."

He went on giving the dispatcher the information of their investigation. His actions, in letting them know where they were and their plan, gave her a certain level of security. Yet, on the other hand, it made her feel more nervous than she had before. Did he think they were going to have a run-in with Shawn? Was he really more concerned with the potential for the curse to come true than he had let on?

The radio quieted and he turned to her. "I want to make it very clear that I think you should stay in the car, but I know you won't. So you need to promise me that you will be careful, okay? Stay behind me. And remember I have a gun, pepper spray, and a Taser. I have everything I need to handle the situation."

"Is that your way of telling me to stay out of your way?" She laughed.

"What can I say? Do I need to remind you about you slipping the gun out of my holster?"

Aura's cheeks warmed. She'd forgotten about stealing his gun. No wonder he was a little bit nervous about taking her into the hotel with him.

"I promise. No gun handling." She crossed her fingers over her heart and held them up like a girl scout.

He smirked wickedly, but said nothing.

"No being dirty. Save it for later." She returned his smile.

His lips turned up in a sexy half grin. "I will."

They got out of the car and he led the way past the automatic doors and into the lobby filled with forest green armchairs. Aura peered into the sitting area, and just like she had imagined, there was a large rock fireplace. Instead of an elk mount, a mountain lion sat perched over the fireplace as if it were looking down upon them like they were prey and it was simply waiting for the right moment to pounce.

She turned back to Dane, who was talking to the woman behind the front desk. He pulled out his wallet and flashed his badge.

"I'd really appreciate if you could tell us the room number and activity for a man named Shawn Gunner."

The lady clicked away at her computer's keyboard, a small frown settled on her face. "I'm sorry, Officer, we don't have anyone staying here by that name."

Dane looked only slightly taken aback, as if part of him knew that Shawn wouldn't be dumb enough to register under his own name with someone else's credit card. "I think they were paying for the room under a credit card owned by a woman named Natalie Montgarten. Can you look it up?"

The woman tapped away again, looking eagerly at the computer as if, as soon as Dane and Aura left the lobby, she would be calling all of her friends to tell them she had been a part of a police investigation. "It looks like we have a Natalie Montgarten registered on the second floor, room 216."

"Thanks," Dane said. "Do you think I can get a key to the room?"

The woman looked at his police-issued black coat. "I don't normally do this," she said, squinting at his silver badge, "Officer Burke..."

"I completely understand," he answered in his most charming voice. "But I'm sure you have heard of the recent murders around Somers. This man is a suspect in the investigation and anything you could do to help us take down the perpetrator would be appreciated, ma'am."

Aura smirked as she listen to the way Dane seemed to use the women's own desire against her. In a strange way, she was almost proud of the man for using his gift for persuasion in the same way she had used her gift for seduction.

"Well, if it's helping your investigation..." The woman grabbed one of the hotel's plastic credit card-like keys and swiped it through the machine. "Here you go. If you need anything else please let me know. I love to help!"

Dane gave her a wide smile and a quick nod as he took the card. "Thanks, ma'am."

Not waiting for him to get done schmoozing the lobby attendant, Aura rushed down the hallway to the little sign that indicated the stairwell. She opened the door and ran up the first five steps as Dane hurried behind her. Her footsteps echoed off the concrete stairs and filled the empty space with their hurried sound.

"Hey, Aura!" he called after her, but there was no slowing her down. "Wait! We can't just go running into the room."

The sound of his voice vibrated down on her, slowing her ascent. He was right. If Natalie was in that room, Shawn wouldn't be likely to give her up easily. And if they weren't careful they could get Natalie hurt. It was better to take their time.

Aura sighed resignedly as she turned and looked down the stairs at Dane. "What do you want to do?"

Taking two stairs at a time, he stepped to her side. "First of all, like I said in the car, you need to stay behind me. I can't protect you if you are in the way. We can't risk you getting hurt."

In the past, she would have refused to acknowledge him taking the lead—she would have barged ahead, taking control of the situation, but this time she stopped. Dane wasn't trying to make her submit, he wasn't trying to control her; instead he was only acting the way he was in an attempt to protect her.

She stepped down so he stood a step in front of her. "I know. I'm sorry."

Dane frowned at her, like he was having trouble reading her intentions. "Are you okay?" He reached up and touched her shoulder.

Aura nodded. "You can take the lead. Let's just get Natalie out of there."

He squeezed his arm. "Honey, you know…it's possible that she won't be in there. And all we have is a video to pin Shawn to her disappearance. In Montana it's almost impossible to prosecute someone unless we find something concrete. The most we will get with the video alone is the ability to take him in for questioning and if we play our cards right, we might be able to get a search warrant for his car."

"She'll be in the room. I just know it. She has to be here." There was marked anxiety in her voice and her heart rose into her throat. What would happen if Natalie wasn't there? If Shawn wasn't really the man they were looking for?

Aura dropped her hand to the stairwell's metal banister as if it could catch her emotions before they threatened to escape her more than they already had.

"I'm sure you're right, honey." Dane dropped his hand and turned up the stairs. "She'll be in there."

She followed behind him the rest of the way to the floor. He opened the door to the second floor and let her pass through ahead of him, but she waited to let him take the lead again. He gave her a strange, concerned look, but said nothing.

The red bordello-reminiscent carpeting dulled the sound of their footsteps that had so loudly announced their presence in the stairwell. The soft crushing sound helped Aura to regain control of her pounding heart. She needed to stay focused if she was going to help Dane.

Time seemed to slow as Aura counted the rooms they passed. 211. 212. 213. 214. 215…216. Her heart rose in her chest. No matter how hard she tried she couldn't stop the way her heart seemed to erratically thrash, almost deafening her with its sound.

Dane put his fingers to his lips, motioning for her to be quiet— as if he too could hear the blood pounding in her ears. He pointed down the hallway a few feet and motioned for her to move back to where he pointed. Aura nodded and moved back about ten feet, so that whoever opened the door couldn't see her without stepping completely out of the hotel door. She pressed her body against the emotionless white wall.

Dane tapped on the wooden door. He tapped again then leaned into the door as if he had heard something and was investigating the sound. Aura tried to silence her heart and hold her breath to listen, but she couldn't hear what he was trying to hear. He motioned for her to come closer.

"I think I hear something inside," he whispered. "Stay out here. Find cover if anything happens."

She nodded. There was nothing around her but more doorways.

With well-practiced precision, Dane pulled the gun at his hip out of its holster and took the ready position, ready to respond at a moment's notice. He quietly slipped the keycard from his pocket and slid it into the lock. The door clicked. He looked back at her with a concerned expression on his face.

"Watch out."

Aura nodded as her heart took on a new racing beat like she was a woman about to step into a war zone.

With a quick push the door flew open.

"Flathead Sheriff's Department! Get down on the ground!" Dane's voice was filled with the force of a man who intended to do whatever was necessary to keep everyone safe. "I repeat, get down on the ground!"

She inched closer to see who Dane was yelling at. As she moved forward Dane made a deep guttural growl-like sound as a man came rushing out the door, bursting past Aura and sprinting down the hallway.

"Get down!" Dane yelled at her, but it was no use, she was frozen to the spot. His words rattled through her like she was a tin can, echoing in her mind, but never really finding a spot to land. All she could do was stare at Shawn as he pulled open the door to the stairs and leapt out of view.

"Shawn! Stop right there!" Dane yelled, as he ran past her after the fleeing suspect. He ripped the Taser from his belt and bolted down the stairs.

The sounds of their running footsteps echoed out from the stairwell and brought Aura back to life. She had to do something. Dane was going after Shawn, but she couldn't stand by and idly watch.

Aura sprinted down the stairs as the woman in the lobby screamed. A gun fired and glass somewhere shattered. Was Dane okay?

Careful of the gunfire, she peered around the doorframe and out into the lobby. The woman was nowhere to be seen and the main room was empty. The glass door leading outside had exploded and glass littered the floor. She pushed out from the stairwell and moved silently against the wall. The woman's rattling sobs from behind the desk filled the tense silence.

Aura moved toward the desk and found the woman lying face down on the ground, unharmed. The woman looked up at her. Her face was pale and almost a light green with fear. "Did they go outside?"

The woman nodded.

Aura looked for something that would work as a weapon, but all that sat on the desk was a computer, printer, and assorted office items. There was nothing she could use to protect herself or Dane. What was she going to do?

Dane's booming voice sounded from outside.

He needed her.

She ran to the smashed door and picked her way through the glass. She followed the sounds of grunts around the side and toward the back parking lot where they had parked the patrol car. There on the ground Shawn was sitting on top of Dane. He lifted his fist and in slow motion she watched as it came down and connected to Dane's nose with a wet muffled sound.

"Stop!" she yelled. "Don't hit him!"

Shawn didn't look back, instead his arm rose. Before he could strike Dane again she ran toward him and grabbed his arm. But he was too strong. His arm slipped through her grip and his fist connected with Dane's face. Blood dripped down from a thick gash over Dane's right eye and his nose was swollen, but unbroken. His eyes were closed and his head bobbed almost lifelessly.

"Goddamn you, Shawn! Stop! You'll kill him!"

She stepped back as Shawn stood up from Dane's unconscious body. There was a gun in his left hand and it moved out of sight as he turned around to face her.

"I've always hated you," he said with a sneer. "You've been nothing but a pain in my ass ever since the first day I met you." He raised his open hand and whipped it across her face with a loud slap. The pain radiated up from her cheek, the sting hot and intense. She reached up and covered the mark with her hands.

"What are you doing? Why are you doing this, Shawn?"

"Just leave me the hell alone, Aura. You and your sister are bitches. Just look at what she did to me." He pointed at his left hand where angry red uneven stitches marked his flesh in the shape of a bite wound.

"But I finally put that bitch in her place." He gave an empty, menacing laugh.

"What did you do to her?"

"*I* didn't do anything." He lifted the gun in his left hand and nonchalantly tossed it into his other hand. He raised the gun halfway and pointed it at Dane's head. "But I'm about to."

She wasn't strong enough to stop him—at least not in her human form. But it had been so long since she'd taken her Mustang form. All the fears that came with her shift returned. She would be vulnerable. And Shawn knew their secret. If he got hold of a single hair she would shift back into her human form. And if he tore out a handful—it would cost her life.

Saving Dane was worth the danger.

The energy coursed through her and instantly her clothes ripped away as her body expanded. It felt strange as her feet shifted into the hooves of her Mustang form. She gave a smile as her face grew longer. The shift was almost immediate. Shawn was going to be a dead man.

Shawn laughed. "You really think you can stop me with your little shift?" He stepped back from her.

She snorted. He would pay.

Aura reared up onto her hind feet, careful to keep her tail away from Shawn's hands. Her hooves flailed through the air as she tried to strike down at the man holding the gun. A groan sounded from Dane and for a moment her concentration wavered.

Dane sat up and looked at her with wide eyes, like he couldn't believe that a palomino Mustang was standing in front of him. She could see the comprehension in his eyes as he wavered on the ground. He knew it was her. He knew she would save them.

Her feet kicked wildly in the air. And Shawn raised the gun up at her. No gun would help him. The shot exploded in the air and ripped through her chest, but she felt nothing—only anger at the man who stood helplessly beneath her.

"Aura no!" Dane yelled, shocking her. But it was too late. Her black left front hoof came down, right on the top of Shawn's collarbone. It snapped with a brittle sound. As her weight came down on his body he crumpled underneath her like she was stomping an empty pop can.

"He may know where Natalie is!" Dane shouted.

She threw her body backwards, careful to not drop her full weight on the already broken man.

Chapter Twenty-One

Aura stood on the other side of the hospital room's window, staring in. Grant and two other officers stood at the entrance to the room, not letting anyone in or out. Shawn had his head down and his restrained arms were pinned behind his back. Dane's head throbbed, but he hadn't let the officer's convince him to hand off the investigation. Grant had been foaming at the mouth, but there wasn't a chance in hell that he was going to let the kid take over the investigation now—not when Dane was so close to getting the answers.

It had been hard to explain the bruises on Shawn's body and the broken clavicle, but the doctors had finally seemed to believe him when he'd explained that he'd taken him to the ground hard.

Aura pulled at her shirt, careful to not let the shirt touch the steadily healing bullet hole in her chest. That was one wound he wouldn't be able to explain to the docs. She should have been dead. The bullet had torn straight through her chest and must have gone straight through her heart.

"He tried to kill me…He wanted to cover his ass…But I didn't kill them…" Shawn dropped his forehead to the white pillow on the hospital bed and cried.

"Who tried to kill you?"

Shawn twisted around, hiding his face. "I didn't kill those women."

Dane lifted the man up off the pillow by the zip ties that were pulled tight around his wrists. "You didn't kill who?"

"Them." Shawn sat like the broken man he was.

"Are you saying you didn't kill Natalie?"

"I didn't kill those women."

"Listen, Shawn. There's no more running, no more fighting—there are only questions and answers from here on out. You need to answer me so that I can understand you. Or else I will let Aura come in here and handle things herself." He pointed out at her. "Now, I'm going to ask you some questions. You are going to give the answers. Get it?"

Shawn stared down at the bed, but nodded.

"Do you know where we can find Natalie Montgarten?"

Shawn jerked. "I told him not to hurt her."

He didn't understand. Was she hurt? Who was "him"? What was Shawn saying?

Aura charged into the door. "Where's Natalie?"

"It's okay, Aura." Dane turned, putting his hand up in a feeble attempt to calm the angry woman. "We'll find out what's going on." He turned back to the man. "Won't we, Shawn? You want to help us, don't you?"

Shawn's eyes glazed over and he said nothing, just began moving back and forth.

"Shawn? Is Natalie alive?" Dane pressed.

"I don't know…" Shawn lurched forward. "She was the last hope we had."

"Who's *we*?"

Shawn moved backward. "I left her with Pat at the Diamond." Dane's heart lurched in his chest.

Natalie was at the Diamond—or at least she had been—if she was still alive. Pat wasn't a man who could be trusted with anything wild and especially not a woman.

"I don't understand. What were you doing with the women in the first place?"

"We needed stronger rodeo stock. The ranch was bleeding money. We had to find a way to make more money."

"How was kidnapping nymphs going to make you more money?"

"We were trying to breed them. Make hybrids. Have horses that were smarter than the average horse, could run faster, but we needed them to not be able to transform back into human—unless we wanted them to."

"You were trying to create mutants?" Aura cried. "What made you think to do something so terrible?"

Shawn lurched back and away from Aura. "It wasn't my idea. Zeb had heard about a nymph giving birth to a hybrid. He and Angela were having problems—were just about to get a divorce. And well, we got us a couple more nymphs. We thought with a few of them we could replicate the results. I mean just think of the money we could make in shows. The horse could do things no dumbass horse could do."

Aura rushed toward the bed, but Dane stuck out his arm and stopped her. "No."

She gave him a look that could have cut glass.

Dane tried to not let her look bother him. She wasn't angry with him, only with the situation. He turned back to the man. "Why did you kill those women? Wouldn't that be counterproductive?"

Shawn ran his hand over the sheet, smoothing down the fabric. "I didn't want Pat to kill them, but when Angela wouldn't listen, he tied her up to his truck and dragged her to the barn. She fought—too hard. We didn't mean to kill her. It was a damned shame—at least to lose Angela. Katarina was a snake-shifter—unfortunately we didn't know there were different shifters until we had a little run-in with her. After that she was of no use to us."

"What about Jenna?" Dane asked, thinking about the last body that they had found.

"She was a swan-shifter. Again, we didn't need her. Our last hope hinged on Natalie."

Dane held back the urge to pick up the man's ugly face and crush his fist into his nose—he owed him one.

"Was Zeb involved in any of this?"

"It was his idea."

Anger poured through him like lava, burning away any last tendrils of empathy he felt for his brother. "You are all going to rot in hell for what you've done to those women."

"They're not women. They're freaks."

• • •

The police had flooded the Diamond. Everyone was there. All available officers from the county had come and even some of the officers from the City of Kalispell. A fire truck sat next to the stables, its red lights swirled on top, bouncing off the snow and creating an otherworldly feel. Next to it sat an ambulance, waiting to be filled with a body—Aura knew that the men standing in wait didn't care whether the body was alive or dead so long as the workers could get out of the cold.

Dane ran his finger over his swollen nose. It looked angry and red, matching the butterfly strip-covered cut over his eye.

"You okay?" Aura asked, moving close to him as she motioned to his nose.

"Fine." He dropped his hands and looked around. "Thanks for *helping out* at the hotel." His gaze shifted around, taking in all the people that flooded the grounds around them.

"You're welcome."

"I know what it meant to you to have to shift…" he whispered. "Especially after everything you've been through. I can't believe you did that for me."

There hadn't been another option. It was either shift or watch him die. "I love you, Dane."

He wrapped his arms around her and pulled her body into him. He pushed his face into her hair. "I love you too."

The sound of a man clearing his throat caught her attention and she pulled out of Dane's arms.

The sergeant stopped a few steps from them. "Sorry, I didn't mean to interrupt anything. I just wanted to let you know we have Pat in custody. He was at the house."

"Where is he?" Dane asked, a dangerous edge to his voice.

"Grant picked him up, was just going to run him in."

"Did he say anything about Natalie?" Aura asked.

"He didn't have anything to say about the whereabouts of Natalie…or Zeb." He looked at Dane. "However, when we ran him in the system we found that Pat is his last name…short for Patrick. His full name's Merle James Patrick. Weren't the initials on the knife you found M. J. P.?"

Dane gave a sharp nod. "Good. That's one bastard who will spend his life behind bars."

Sergeant Tester nodded. "That makes two. About number three, do you have any idea where your brother would be hiding?"

"We've searched the entire place, but if he went up into the woods there's no telling when he'll come out. Or if he'll come back."

The cows in the pasture that ran to the left of the road looked over at them, giving Aura an idea. Maybe one of the animals could help, but there was no way she could use her ability in front of the throngs of officers and emergency workers—unless she was careful.

As the men discussed the case, Aura weaved past the people that stood around the corral and stables. At the far end of the horse stalls Dancer stuck his head out of the door, watching all the people almost as if they were a show that played out in front of him.

She walked toward him, grabbing a pellet from the bucket that hung from a hook on the wall. "Hello, handsome," she said in a smooth, easy voice.

His energy wavered with all the noise and commotion going on around him, but his curiosity kept him from running back into the corner of the stall and hiding like several of the other horses had done. His black silky coat was velvety under her fingers as she ran her hands down over his nose and them up to his mane.

We are looking for Zeb…Do you know where he's gone?

Dancer looked at her, his attention finally breaking from the mass of people and energies that flowed around them. *Zeb?* he answered. *The one who smells like poison?*

She couldn't think of a man who smelled like poison. Was there something she had missed?

What do you mean, honey? Poison?

You know, the black poison he stuffs under his lip.

Aura smiled as she realized the horse was talking about the snuff that Zeb habitually chewed.

Yes, the poison man. Have you seen him?

Dancer brought his head up with an agitated jerk, but she kept her hands on him, careful to not break the connection. *He was here. He had a rope in his hands… Then he disappeared…*

He had a rope? What had he been doing? Was he planning on hurting himself? Or was the rope to hurt Natalie? The image of Angela's disarticulated hand screamed through her mind.

If Zeb was running from them then he had to know that they had found out the truth…that he was guilty of participating in the abduction and murder of several women—and the gods only knew what he would be thinking. He had much to lose— the ranch, his image, and maybe even his life. He hadn't thought anything of killing those women, nothing would stop him from killing Natalie now—*if* she was still alive.

She had to hurry. *Where did he disappear? Did he leave the barn?*

No. Dancer huffed with agitation and he jerked his head in the direction of the stall that sat empty across the aisle. *He went in there.*

Not an hour before, she'd watched Dane walk through the stalls, finding nothing. *Are you sure?*

Dancer gave her a look of subtle annoyance.

Sorry. She smiled. *Thank you for your help.*

Dancer leaned against the door and laid his head on her shoulder. *No, thank you for your help. You saved me.*

She hugged his neck softly. *I just hope I can keep helping you.*

With Zeb going to prison it wasn't likely that he would be back to the ranch. Dancer would be at the mercy of the courts—he would be sold to some stranger and an unknown fate. The thought drew a tear to her eye. She'd saved him once, but it was unlikely she could be so lucky again.

"Aura, you okay?" Dane asked, breaking the bond between her and Dancer.

She ran her hand down Dancer's face and stepped back. "I'm okay," she lied. "I think I might know where we can find Zeb." She pointed at the empty stall.

"I was just in there. There's nothing." Dane smiled.

"Trust me." She motioned slightly toward Dancer.

"Oh…" He stared at the horse. "Thanks, Dancer," he whispered, careful not to be heard.

Aura stepped to the empty stall and opened the door. The floor was covered in fresh hay. The wooden walls were plain white, the same as every other stall. There was nothing amiss or out of place.

"Was he sure?" Dane glanced at Dancer, almost with disbelief that she could communicate with the beautiful black gelding.

She reached over and took his hand. "There are some things in life that you can trust to tell you the truth. Animals don't lie. Their body tells you everything you need to know. It's just that humans have never learned how to listen."

She shuffled her feet around in the hay, making a wide square that grew tighter and tighter until her foot slid over a hole in the floor. "Dane! I think I found something."

Bending over, she rifled through the straw, exposing a metal handle entrenched in a shallow indentation. Dane stepped over to her and reached down and lifted up the handle, exposing a small wooden ladder.

He looked at her. "You need to be careful. Please. I've got a bad feeling."

"If anyone between us needs to be careful, it's you. You've been hurt too much. Maybe you should stay up here and let me go."

"Aura," he said tiredly, "I'm a *deputy*. This is my job. You can't constantly be worrying that I'll get hurt."

"If you are going to be with me, you are just going to have to get used to someone who cares about you, who loves you and wants you to be safe."

He took her hand and gave it a squeeze. "I love you too." He put his foot down onto the top rung of the ladder. Dane let go of her as he disappeared into the darkness.

Her hands shook as she followed him into the shadows. She would have to trust his gut and what he thought was best. Her foot struck the dirt floor and she let go of the ladder. It took her a second to let her eyes adjust to the enveloping darkness of the cellar-like basement.

"Zeb?" Dane called out. "Are you in here?"

They were answered with the footsteps of the people walking in the barn above them.

He pulled his gun from his holster and stepped in front of her. Her heart thundered in her ears. If Zeb was down here, was he alive? Was he with Natalie? If she was down here why wasn't she answering? A sickening knot clenched tight in her stomach and a wave of chills made goose bumps rise on her arms. Something was wrong.

"Natalie?" she called out, her voice wavering with emotion.

Again there was no answer.

Dane pulled the work-issued metal flashlight from its holster at his side and shined the light into the murky black. At the far end of the square room was a wall and at its center was a barn wood door that sat half off its hinges.

She looked over at him. "How long has this place been down here?"

Dane shook his head. "This wasn't here before the barn burned…It's only been a few years—at least that I know about."

Was it possible that his family had more secrets under their barn than most did in their closet? Were there things his mother hadn't told him?

She moved meticulously toward the door, step by step with Dane.

He stepped ahead and the door's hinges cried in rusty anger at their intrusion. A low watt yellow-tinted light hung from an electrical wire strung from the ceiling. Something else moved in the darkness just beyond the thin light.

"What's that?" Aura felt the energy of her shift begin to course through her body, but she tried to control it, put it back in the little box where it had, for so long before today, been trapped.

Dane pointed his flashlight in the direction of the movement. Squinting she moved closer.

"No…" She gasped.

The light reflected off a pair of clean camel-colored boots at the level of her waist.

"Zeb…What did you do?" The metal flashlight fell to the floor as Dane rushed to his dangling brother.

She picked up the light and pointed it toward the rafter which the green and yellow rope was tied. Her mind flipped to the crime lab's report on Angela's body—they had found yellow and green fibers—rope fibers. Zeb had been behind it all. She moved the light down, illuminating the purple flesh of Zeb's lifeless face. She gasped. Dane didn't deserve this, to find his brother like this. Not here. Not in this place. He already had so many terrible memories tied to this barn.

A whimper escaped from the darkness. Aura flashed the light around the room. In the far corner, stuck against the wall, was a wooden chair. At first all she could see were the duct-taped legs, but as she moved closer, her sister's face met her. Her eyes were closed from the sudden intensity of the flashlight's beam.

"Natalie!" She ran to her.

Her sister's normally beautiful dark chestnut-colored hair was matted with dirt and sweat and hung limply to her face, making Aura's heart ache in her chest. She'd been through so much.

"It's okay, honey. I'm here." The duct tape was stuck firmly over her lips, but Aura was careful as she pulled it from Natalie's lips. "Are you okay?"

"Aura!" Tears slipped down Natalie's dirt-smudged cheeks. "I didn't think you were ever going to find me. I'm...I'm so sorry."

"No...I'm sorry." Aura took Natalie in her arms, comforting her still trapped body.

She couldn't stop the tears that welled in her eyes and spilled down her face. Every emotion she had been feeling—terror, dread, love, excitement, and elation—every emotion filled her tears and poured from her. She'd never felt such relief. Natalie was safe. She was alive. There would be scars for many years to come, but she was still here on this earth—Aura could ask nothing more.

"I should have never let you come here alone. If I hadn't been so wrapped up in my own life...this would have never happened." Tears choked her voice.

Natalie moved as if she wanted to hug her, but her arms were still taped behind her back. "Aura, this wasn't your fault. I'm just so glad you're here."

"Natalie?" Dane asked, stepping to Aura's side. "I'm so glad you're okay. We were worried about you." There was a strangled edge to his voice, as if his emotions threatened to spill over.

Aura pulled at the thick wrap of tape around Natalie's ankles. "Dane, do you have a knife?" He reached to his waist and pulled out a well-worn knife. Bending down, he made quick work of the tape then moved behind the chair and repeated the action with Natalie's wrists.

He gently moved Natalie's hands around to her lap. "Are you okay?"

"I think so—at least I think I'll be okay." Natalie nodded as she rubbed the skin of her wrists. "Who are you?"

"I'm Deputy Burke."

"But you can call him Dane." Aura smiled as she thought of the first moment she'd met him as he stood by her window, trying his damnedest to be the hard-edged cop, but she knew the real him—the man who could love without boundaries, without care of his safety, and with the full strength of his being.

"That's right…You can call me Dane." Dane glanced up at her and smiled, as if he too was thinking of that fateful moment.

Natalie wiped the tears from her face. "Thank you, Dane… Aura…Thank you for finding and saving me."

Chapter Twenty-Two

Natalie peered out the window of Aura's truck as they made their way from the hospital to Dane's house. Some of the pink hues of life had returned to her cheeks and her body had taken on a new life, as if she knew how lucky she was to be alive.

Her beautiful copper-tinted brown locks flowed perfectly over her shoulders, framing her petite face. For everything that she had gone through, it was incredible to see how much better she had looked from the pale-faced, dirt-covered woman they'd pulled from the cellar only a week before.

"Are you sure you were ready to be discharged? You could have stayed a little while longer," Aura offered as she tried almost in vain to focus on the road.

"No, it was time. I want to get out and Ryan's waiting. Plus, I could really use a run."

"You mean shift?"

Natalie passed her a guilty grin, but Aura couldn't blame her. It came as no surprise that her sister would want to return to her horse form as soon as possible. She seemed so much more at home as the beautiful chestnut-colored mare.

"What are you going to do, Aura?" Natalie pushed her hair away from her face. "Are you going to head back to Arizona?"

The whir of the tires on the highway filled the cab. She hadn't made a plan. For so long, all she had worried about was finding Natalie, but for the last week she had been considering their options for the future. They would head back to Arizona—go back to work training horses and saving more wild Mustangs from slaughter, but her heart sank in her chest every time she considered leaving Dane.

She loved him with every fiber of her being, and leaving him would be the hardest thing she would ever have to do; yet their money was running dry. They needed work, but more importantly she still needed to keep Dane safe. He had heard the warning and he'd lived through Shawn and fate's attempts to kill him—but the blows wouldn't stop coming as long as she was in his life. If she loved him she had to walk away—and even the thought threatened to kill her.

Aura tried to ignore the aching throb in her chest. "I bet you want to get out of Montana?"

"What do you mean?" Natalie answered in an overly chipper voice.

Aura gave her a forced sardonic grin. "You don't have to fake anything with me. I know how hard this has all been on you, how hard it would be to stay here and be confronted with the memories of your horrific ordeal."

Natalie fidgeted in her seat for a second. "Actually, it might surprise you, but it hasn't all been bad here. I found a little bit of a silver lining."

Sometimes her sister still surprised her. Few people—or nymphs for that matter—could come through a kidnapping and witnessing multiple murders and still be focused on the bright side of life. Perhaps there was something to be said for her softhearted, Bohemian-styled sister.

"I found something for you and Dane…A bit of a thank you present."

"Natalie, you didn't have to get us anything. I'm just glad that you're back. I don't know what I would have done without you."

Her sister smiled. "From what I can see you've done pretty well on your own. Dane's a great man. You did good."

"I think so…" She tried to sound happy, but the fears that lingered in her heart filled her voice with ghostly reservation.

She pulled the truck to a stop in front of Dane's house. A fresh layer of perfectly white snow blanketed the ground, freshening the world around them. Ryan had crutches under his arms as he stood next to Dane beside the door as they both waited for the women to arrive. A sexy, wanting smile played on Dane's lips. She hated herself for what she was going to have to do.

Natalie jumped out and sprinted to Ryan, throwing her arms around him. "Ryan! Did you tell Dane yet?"

Ryan gave her a wide smile. "Not yet. I was waiting for you."

Natalie pulled from Ryan's arms and turned to Dane and gave him a hearty hug. "Hey, little Danish! Long time no see."

He looked taken aback, but his normally stoic face broke into a wide smile as Aura slogged to the front door. "I'm glad you're feeling better." He gave Natalie a quick squeeze before she fluttered out of his arms and helped Ryan walk into the house.

Ryan hobbled into the house as the lively Natalie moved through the living room. "This is a really great place you've got."

"Thanks," Dane called after Natalie. He waited for Aura to step beside him. "She seems a lot better."

"So does Ryan. I'm glad it was only a broken leg." She forced herself to give him a weak smile. "Natalie always has been the one to keep moving forward. She's always looking around the bend for the next adventure. It's one of the best parts of being a wild mare."

"She's amazing, but so are you." He wrapped his fingers in hers and walked with her into the house, shutting the door behind them. Natalie was down the hall, already making herself at home as she looked over his collection of pictures.

"I think you need some new pictures, Danish." Natalie picked up the picture of him and Zeb and made a sour face. "Ryan, did you see this? I mean, I'm as sorry as I can be about your brother's death and all, but I don't think he needs to see these anymore. Don't you agree, Ryan?" She sat the picture face down on the shelf.

Ryan gave Dane an apologetic smile, as if he knew Natalie was overextending her welcome.

"Natalie…" Aura's cheeks flamed with her sister's brashness.

The funeral had been a county-wide event; not for Zeb's memory, but more as a show of support for Dane and all that he'd gone through with his family.

"No, Natalie's right." Dane squeezed her hand as he smiled. "I think I'm going to move out."

"What?" Aura couldn't believe it. What was he thinking? "Are you going to just buy another place?"

She could understand his desire to find a new home, somewhere that didn't have Angela's phantom touch.

"Actually…I have some great news." His smile grew. "The woman who owns the property next to the Diamond, Mrs. Mullen, has agreed to buy the ranch and this property. She's paying more than it's worth—enough for me to retire very comfortably. In fact, there's enough for us all to never have to worry again."

"Dane…" Aura's hands flew up and covered her mouth. "No… We can't. You can't sell the ranch."

"It's already done." He walked to the kitchen and picked up a paper-filled yellow file. "It's all taken care of. And every horse in the place has found a new fabulous home, under the care of Mrs. Mullen and her family. All except one." His smile grew even wider. "She said she couldn't handle Dancer…He's too much horse for her. She required that he find a great trainer who was willing to take him in."

Aura rushed to him and threw her arms around his neck. "Thank you so much." If nothing else, she would have a wonderful horse to remember all the great times that she had spent with Dane—and their night in the snow.

He dropped the file on the counter and wrapped his arms around her. "I love you, sweetheart."

Ryan moved to the sofa and, setting down his crutches, dropped down on the couch.

Dane looked over to him. "And Ryan, you are welcome to come along too. We can start up a new place, wherever we end up."

"Thanks, Dane…That's mighty gracious of you." Ryan smiled. "I mean…especially after my Dad and all. I'm real sorry about him…and what he did."

Dane looked down at Aura as if he was waiting for her to answer Ryan, but it was unnecessary—she held no ill-feelings toward the man who loved her sister.

"If Natalie loves you and you love her, then that is the most important thing." *Or the most dangerous.* But to love him was her sister's decision to make.

Dane leaned back in her arms. "I do have one condition to all of this."

Her heart lurched in her chest. "What?"

"You have to marry me. We can go anywhere you want. Back to Arizona…anywhere."

"What about your job? You love your job."

"I can be a cop anywhere. Plus, I'm looking forward to getting away from Grant. There's nothing here for me anymore—only some burned out memories." He dropped down to his knees and pulled a small black velvet box from his pocket.

Her breath caught in her throat and the world spun around her.

"I never thought I would do this again, but I can't live without you, Aura Montgarten. You are everything that I've ever wanted. Please, will you marry me?"

She smiled her best smile, even though her heart was breaking. "Dane," she said as she dropped her hands to the box and forced it closed. "Thank you for your generous offer, but you and I...We can't—"

"Can't what?" Natalie interrupted. "Are you crazy? Marry him!"

Aura blinked as she tried desperately to focus on her sister's face and not the world that spun around her. "Nat, you know the curse. I can't do that. I love him too much."

Natalie's laugh flew through the room like a perky yellow canary as she reached into the pocket of her jeans. "I told you I had a surprise!" She pulled out her hand and uncurled her fingers. Sitting in the middle of her palm was a small blue crystal-like stone.

"A rock is your surprise?" Aura asked, utterly confused.

"Don't you remember?" Natalie rolled her eyes. "Katarina Homeros...Yes?"

Aura nodded, recalling the murdered woman from Crete. "What about her?"

Natalie stepped over and slipped the sky-colored stone beneath the black velvet box in Dane's quaking hand. "Do you remember what she did?"

Aura paused as she recalled the history of their kind—the Goddess Epione's ill-fated run-in with Zeus and Katarina's role in hiding her healing staff...The staff that Katarina had broken.

"It isn't?" Aura stared down at the chip of stone in Dane's hand.

Natalie excitedly skipped from one foot to another, like a prancing horse. "It is! It's a piece of Epione's staff. Katarina kept talking about her and Ariadne...and just before she died she entrusted me with it."

Aura stood in stunned silence, her fingers still touching Dane's warm, open hand. They could have one another. They could have love. They could escape the curse.

"What about you and Ryan?" Aura asked, trying to control her heart from exploding in her chest.

Natalie smiled guiltily and pointed toward Ryan. "Show her."

Ryan stuck out his hand and held out a small blue stone that matched Dane's.

"I broke it in half. We can both have what we've always wanted…" Natalie wiggled with visible joy.

Dane looked at Aura with a look of confusion. "What are you talking about?"

"Our kind was created by Epione, the goddess of soothing pain and healing. She's why we can heal ourselves. She had a staff." Aura's fingers traced the blue stone in his hand. "It was broken, but the pieces still hold the power of the staff. Those who hold it cannot be killed. As long as you and Ryan keep this stone you will not die."

He stroked her fingers with his thumb and smiled up at her. "You're saying we can be together forever?"

She nodded wildly. Aura couldn't speak as the tears of relief and joy flooded from her.

"Then will you please marry me?"

Dropping to her knees, Aura opened the black velvet box. The light danced over the surface of the beautiful solitary diamond that rested in the center of the perfect gold band.

"Dane…We can…I do…I will."

She'd always thought she was free, yet at that moment, as Dane slipped the ring upon her finger, she knew the truth—she'd never been truly free until now. For the first time in her immortal life she was free to love.

A Sneak Peek from Crimson Romance
(From *The Nymph's Labyrinth* by Danica Winters)

The Palace of Knossos, Crete 1613 BCE

Zeus stepped to the side of the bed and lifted the sheet to gaze at Epione's sleeping form. The goddess' hair splayed around her head in a black halo and her hands rested over her bare breasts. The warm ocean breeze filtered through the curtains behind him as he stared down at her tanned chest while it rose and fell with the innocence of sleep.

The air must have startled her and she stirred. The nymph's hands shifted from her breasts as she moved to stretch, and the action made the God's manhood quiver to life. He dropped the sheets back down and as the air wafted against her skin, she opened her eyes. "Hmmm. Zeus?" She yawned. "Have you come to me in need of healing?"

Epione sat up, pushed her legs out from beneath the bedding and stood up. Zeus' gaze fell to her round breasts and trailed down to the black wavy hair between her thighs. "I come for deeper needs. Needs only a woman…no, only a nymph can fill."

She stumbled toward her robe that lay draped over the wooden chair at the end of the bed, but he put out his arm, stopping her. "You won't be in need of a covering."

She glared at him as she backed away from his touch, and bumped against the wooden bed behind her. "What of your wife? She'll be angry if you stray from your marriage bed, will she not?" Epione pulled her hair over her shoulders and covered her chest.

"Are you not the goddess of all nymphs? The Queen of the seductresses? Is it not your job to soothe a man? I am here to be a victim of your seduction, to have the needs of my manhood and my aching desires sated by your touch, not to worry about the fickle emotions of my wife."

"A man who treats his wife with such indifference will find no place in my bed. I believe in true love, not infidelity."

"She cares not where I plant my seed—only that I return to her." Zeus reached out to touch her. "Come here and show me how you seduce, then I will leave and you can find another man who you can *love*."

He laughed at the thought of such a romantic idea. Who wouldn't want a nice tussle without the attachments of love? And the Queen of seduction? She would most certainly be in need of good lovemaking. He would love to teach her the ways of a real God.

Epione stared up at him with her bright green eyes. She was even more beautiful than the other gods of Olympus had foretold.

"I know who you are, and of your erotic escapades. I wish only to be made wet by those who love me eternally, not those who wish to ravish me for sake of their fantasies." Epione turned to the bed, grabbed a sheet and pulled it around her. "I seduce and soothe whom I choose."

Zeus ran his fingers along the edge of the white sheet, so close to her breasts. So close to possessing what his loins called for. Her denial only made him want it more. "I am a God. I have sired gods and goddesses, and ruled humankind. Having me as a lover is an honor. There's no reason you should not choose me." He leaned closer to her, and could smell the salty scent of her skin. "My body is ravaged with pain of want and only you can dampen my fire."

He followed her gaze toward the corner of the room, where a crystal staff shimmered in the sun, but he cared nothing of her trinkets, only the purpose that pulsed from between his thighs.

She sat down on the edge of the bed, careful to keep her body covered. "You'll need to find another to wet your fire."

Anger flashed within him. *Who does she think she is?*

He reached toward her, but she pushed his hand away. "I am a god. The *God* of gods. I ravish whomever I desire. My touch is an honor to those with whom I share my bed."

With a calm fury, she flung aside the sheets, pushed up from the bed and sidestepped around him. He turned as he watched her grab the crystal staff.

She glared at him with a fury reminiscent of the fires of Hades. "Let me be the first to be dishonored."

Zeus stepped back and lightening sparked from his fingers. His body responded with a hardness that came to the men of war. "I will not beg. You'll give me what I want, or I will take it."

Epione thrust the staff in the direction of his manhood. "Come near me and I'll burn it off."

He covered his groin and sneered. "Your denial will bring only acrimonious dishonor."

"So be it." She jabbed the staff at him again.

He glared at the idealistic goddess. "Because of you, your kind will be cursed. Never again will you or your kind partake in your senseless desire for *true love*. If a nymph attempts to love a human, that man will be fated to die a tragic death!"

"No." The crystal staff lowered as she shirked from his words.

He raised his arms to the sky and bellowed. The ground quaked beneath him. "This island and everything you hold dear I condemn to the fires of Thera. All because you dared to turn a god away!"

"You wouldn't!" she cried. "What of the humans?"

"The Minoans worship the bull, not the God of gods. They deserve no mercy."

The walls cracked and fissured around them as the earth shook. Thunder filled the air and from the window, a cloud of gray ash poured from the direction of the volcano to the North.

"Foolish Epione, you and all that your humans hold dear will this day be destroyed."

In the mood for more Crimson Romance?
Check out *Rhapsody*
by Sharon Clare
at *CrimsonRomance.com*.

About the Author

Danica Winters is a bestselling author who is known for writing award-winning books that grip readers with their ability to drive emotion through suspense and often a touch of magic. When she's not working, she can be found in the wilds of Montana testing her patience while she tries to understand the allure of various crafts (quilting, pottery, and painting are not her thing). She always believes the cup is neither half full nor half empty, but it better be filled with wine.

Please feel free to contact her through her website:

www.DanicaWinters.net
Or on Facebook: *www.Facebook.com/DanicaWinters*
Or Twitter: *www.Twitter.com/DanicaWinters*

Printed in the United States
By Bookmasters